THE SPIRIT

OF THE

SEASON

A Lexie Starr Mystery

Novella

Jeanne Glidewell

*Author proceeds from the sale of this book are donated
directly to Toys for Tots.
Thank you for your generous support.*

Cover and Book design by eBook Prep www.ebookprep.com

First Edition, November 2013
ISBN: 978-1-61417-498-1

ePublishing Works!
www.epublishingworks.com

DEDICATION

This short Lexie Starr holiday novella is dedicated to all the members and past members of the military, and their families. The family members holding down the fort at home, while their loved ones are deployed overseas, deserve a lot of credit, acknowledgement, and gratitude for all they sacrifice while their spouse, parent or child serve to protect our freedom. As a token of my personal appreciation, I am pledging to donate all the proceeds from the sale of this novella to the Leavenworth, Kansas, Chapter of the Toys for Tots program. Founded in 1947, the Toys for Tots program is run by the United States Marine Corps Reserve. I hope readers will consider donating an unwrapped toy, or two, to their local Toys for Tots Chapters, which benefit many underprivileged families and helps them to all have a merrier holiday season.

FOREWORD

As the Coordinator of the Leavenworth, Kansas, Toys for Tots program, I'm directly involved with every aspect of it, including fundraising, collections, and distributing toys to qualified families. I've been in the Marine Corps for nine years, and am currently classified as a Sergeant. I work as a Correctional Specialist, and am stationed at Fort Leavenworth, serving as a Marine Liaison at the United States Disciplinary Barracks, the maximum-security prison for the military. My involvement with the Toys for Tots program is a welcome diversion, and as a 27-year-old, single mother of 3-year-old son, Logan, it's a rewarding mission that's dear to my heart.

Each year as the holiday season approaches, most families begin to prepare for Christmas around October. Unfortunately, there are people who can't afford to give their children gifts to wake up to Christmas morning, which can cause depression and stressful holidays for the entire family. Sadly, there are many families such as this in the military and in our own neighborhoods. As mentioned in Jeanne Glidewell's Lexie Starr holiday novella, *The Spirit of the Season,* there are ways you can help, by adopting an underprivileged family, or contributing to local organizations like the Marine Corps Toys for Tots program each year.

The Marine Toys for Tots Foundation began in 1947 when Major Bill Hendricks, and the Marine Reservists collected over 5,000 toys and distributed them to disadvantaged families. Major Hendricks's wife, Diane, had wanted to donate a handcrafted Raggedy Ann doll to a needy child for Christmas and discovered there was no existing agency that served this purpose. She encouraged her husband to create such an organization, which he did.

Major Hendricks's new Toys for Tots program was so successful that year that the United States Marine Corps adopted the program in 1948, and expanded it into a nationwide annual campaign. Each year the Marine Corps Reserve raise funds and display collection boxes inside retail stores who help sponsor the program, such as Lexie Starr does in this mystery novella. People can donate an unwrapped toy or two that are usually no more than ten dollars in value. The toys are collected weekly and stored until December when they are distributed to families in need of assistance.

Donations can also be made to your local chapters through the website, www.toysfortots.org. Likewise, families in need can sign up through their local Assistance Center for approval.

The Leavenworth Chapter of the Toys for Tots program would like to thank Jeanne Glidewell, who will be donating all the proceeds of *The Spirit of the Season* novella to this chapter. Our gratitude for her kindness and generosity in doing so goes far beyond words. We'd also like to express our appreciation to all the organizations and local citizens for their yearly donations, which help make our program so successful.

Please help spread the word about this program, and consider making an annual donation yourself, so we can all work together to bring joy to as many underprivileged children as possible each holiday season.

Sgt. Dominique G. Yost, USMC
Photo by Hayden Photography

ACKNOWLEDGEMENTS

I'd like to thank my talented editor, Judy Beatty, of Madison, Alabama, for tracking down phantom commas that sneak onto the pages when I'm not looking. In the true American spirit of caring and giving, Judy is also donating her time and editing skills to the Toys for Tots program, and her generosity is very much appreciated. For editing services, you can contact her at judyedits4u@gmail.com.

I'd also like to thank Brian and Nina Paules, of ePublishing Works, and eBook Prep, for allowing me to spend my time writing while they expertly take care of the details of publishing my digital and print books.

And, last, but not least, I'd like to thank Sergeant Dominique Yost for her help with this novella, and for providing the forward for *The Spirit of the Season*.

The Lexie Star Mystery series is available in print eBook. Excerpts can be found at the end of this novella.

CHAPTER 1

My mother always told me I should learn something new every day. Today, I learned you couldn't microwave a potato for fifty-five minutes without causing a small kitchen fire. And throwing a bag's worth of flour at it only leaves you five pounds of flour to clean up off the floor and stove, after you've cleaned up the mess left by the fire.

I'm Alexandria Marie Starr, or Lexie to everyone but my mother, who was very proud of the name she'd picked for me and refused to shorten it for the sake of convenience. My husband of six months, Stone Van Patten, and I own a bed and breakfast establishment called the Alexandria Inn in the small town of Rockdale, Missouri. I am currently filling in as the interim head librarian at the local library, a temporary job I took to cure my boredom while a seasonal slump slowed business at the inn.

After an enjoyable day of working at the Rockdale Public Library, I was at the Inn preparing supper for

Stone and me, along with a younger couple who were currently guests of the inn. The Harringtons were from Wyoming, and the RV Park they owned in Cheyenne was closed for the winter. They were staying at the inn while visiting family during their vacation.

I had decided to "bake" some potatoes in the microwave while Stone grilled rib eye steaks out on the grill. When my daughter, Wendy, who would turn thirty soon, called me on the telephone, I was too fixated on my conversation with her to pay attention to the cooking time I was setting on the microwave, and didn't realize I'd screwed up until smoke began bellowing out from the exhaust vent. When I opened the door of the smoldering microwave in panic, the charred potatoes erupted into flames.

I shouted out my husband's name while simultaneously grabbing the flour canister and flinging it wildly at the rapidly expanding fire. I don't know where I'd gotten the idea that flour could extinguish a nuked-to-death potato-induced fire. The ceramic canister shattered into pieces as five pounds of flour floated down like snow on Christmas Eve, covering nearly every square inch of the stovetop, floor, and sink. Pretty much the only thing the flour missed was the microwave, which Stone later told me was probably a stroke of good fortune because it may have only helped fuel the fire.

While I watched flames flickering off the cherry wood cabinet above the microwave, Stone rushed in and put the fire out with a fire extinguisher that hung on the wall about two feet from where I'd been standing when I first noticed the smoke. I was usually better than this in a crisis.

If nothing else, I was now pretty much assured of receiving the new combination microwave/convection oven that I'd been eyeing at Nebraska Furniture Mart for months, as a Christmas present from Stone, who always stressed out when faced with selecting a gift for me.

This new oven would be a vast improvement over the Hobb's Creek fly-fishing rod and reel outfit, and neoprene chest waders Stone had given me for my birthday. He'd been determined to make a fisherwoman out of me, and I tried my best to comply with his wishes. Stone's idea of heaven was wandering around a Bass Pro Shop store with a one-hundred-dollar gift card to spend.

My dear husband had been consumed with delight as we drove to Bennett Springs for our first trout-fishing trip last spring. We settled into our rental cabin, ate a hearty breakfast, and headed to the Niangua River to catch some rainbow trout. After my first cast resulted in twenty-five yards of fishing line wrapped around me in an almost unbelievable rat's nest, and a hand-tied fly's hook hopelessly embedded in Stone's shirt collar, his determination to make a fisherwoman out of me waned a bit.

When nearly every cast that followed ended up in a similar tangled mess, Stone's dream was snuffed entirely, and I was never asked to go fishing with him again. He returned my birthday presents to the sporting goods store the next day, and I picked out some really cute shirts and blue jean shorts to replace them.

"Mom? Hello? Mom, are you there?" My daydreaming was interrupted when I heard my daughter's voice emitting from the phone that I'd dropped on the floor when I'd noticed the smoke. She had a frantic tone to her voice, no doubt caused by my piercing scream and the sound of a ceramic canister disintegrating. The next thing she probably heard was Stone asking me if I wanted the steaks as well done as the potatoes.

My day had started with a cup of coffee on the back porch of the inn, where I loved to read the *Rockdale Gazette* that Howie Clamm faithfully flung into the thorny bushes at the end of our circle driveway at precisely five o'clock every morning. It was an unseasonably warm day for early November and my ratty Kansas City Chiefs sweatshirt was all I needed to keep me comfortable while I read the paper as I relaxed on a chaise lounge. Our small town newspaper contained a lot of advertisements, several pages of local gossip, a few editorials written by extremely incensed and opinionated citizens, and very little actual news.

If you wanted to know who ate lunch with whom the previous day, this was the place to look. Pansy Paxton, a part-time contributor who penned the daily *Pansy's Place* column, was right on top of everything that happened in town, no matter how insignificant.

This particular morning I learned that Opal Wittenhauer's sister, who was celebrating her ninetieth birthday, would be coming to visit the following Saturday, which incidentally, was the last day of the local farmer's market this season. Another tidbit of fascinating news I garnered from Pansy's column was that Hazel Hallberg's Bear Claw patterned quilt had sold for a pretty penny at the silent auction held by the Lion's Club last Friday night.

The most newsworthy item in the entire paper was about a group of boys playing in the city park who had shot a glass globe off an antique lamppost with a pellet gun. A similar incident had occurred the previous week and the city council was calling a special session to discuss the situation. I passed this information on to Stone who soon joined me on the back porch, and he couldn't have been less interested. In the last couple of years, the most sensational articles in the *Gazette* had featured a mug of me on the front page, accompanied by a story of how my clever investigative techniques, or at least my incredible good luck and uncanny timing, had helped solve a murder case and brought a killer to justice.

Following in Stone's wake, out on to the back porch,

was Detective Wyatt Johnston, a fifteen-year veteran of the Rockdale Police Department. He had become a close friend of ours due to my habit of becoming personally involved in the investigations of several local murder cases, two of which had occurred at the Alexandria Inn during its first year of operation.

Detective Johnston is six-and-a-half feet of muscle-bound masculinity, and he could consume ten thousand calories a day without gaining an ounce, unlike Stone and I who were both under-tall, and slightly overweight. The latter I blamed on the detective. If I didn't have to keep plenty of sweet pastries on hand to offer him, I'm sure I would be better able to retain my ideal weight.

As was nearly always the case, Wyatt was carrying a cup of coffee in one hand, and a chocolate long john in the other. Since becoming a frequent guest at the inn, he had become almost as addicted to caffeine as I was. My addiction was so severe that Stone had warned me that eventually the fingers of my right hand would be permanently curled in the cup-handle-carrying position.

"Howdy, Lexie! How's it going?" Wyatt asked, as he sat down on a patio chair next to me.

"Great! But I'm surprised you had time to stop by this morning. I thought you'd be tied up investigating the pellet gun crime spree."

"Yeah, right," he said. "It's kind of sad that in this sleepy little town something like that is about as exciting as our police work gets. Unless, of course, you, my dear Lexie Starr, are knee deep in distress while butting into a murder investigation."

"Hey! Hand over that long john that I bought especially for you, right this second! Not another bite until you take back that remark, and, furthermore, all future pastries will be put on hold until you apologize!" I demanded good-naturedly as I yanked the doughnut out of his hand.

"Sorry, Lexie. I didn't mean to say that, or at least not

out loud anyway," Wyatt replied with a smile. "I know your investigative skills have proved to be very beneficial in solving several of Rockdale's most wicked crimes. The word 'skills' may be a little overblown, but your efforts *have* been effective in the past. Now may I please have my long john back?"

After finishing my third cup of coffee, I left Stone and Wyatt to discuss ice-fishing augers while I went upstairs to dress for work and try to perform a miracle by making my short, curly, light-brown hair presentable to the public. It was Friday, and after cooking breakfast for the Harringtons, I needed to report to the library at nine o'clock to execute my head librarian duties.

The Alexandria Inn is a first class lodging facility. Our bed and breakfast business revolves around pampering our guests well beyond what is expected from an establishment such as ours. Dinner, as well as breakfast, is provided for our guests, as are personalized services such as transportation, museum, antique shop, and historic home tours, catered family reunions, and anything else we can do to make their stay enjoyable. Our business depended on good word-of-mouth advertising, and so far our strategy had paid off. The bed and breakfast had proved to be a very successful endeavor.

Several weddings, including ours, have been held on the premises, with the nuptials taking place in the gazebo Stone built in the center of the rose garden, adjacent to the massive historic Victorian mansion that we'd renovated to create the Alexandria Inn. The food for these special events has always been provided by a catering business in town. Knowing the mess I can make just nuking a spud, you can surely see why I leave cooking for the masses to the professionals.

I fried some eggs to serve with french toast and bacon for breakfast. The eggs were a little too runny, the french toast a little too soggy, and the bacon a little too crisp, but the Harringtons didn't seem to mind. They were planning to spend the day with her parents in St. Joseph, which was not far from Rockdale.

After clearing off the dining room table, and cleaning the kitchen, I kissed Stone goodbye, handed Wyatt another doughnut, and headed out to my pale yellow Volkswagen Beetle, that I recently purchased after my nearly new blue sports car got blown to smithereens. The drive to the library took less than two minutes, including a red light at Fourth and Locust Street.

CHAPTER 2

My workday started off with the routine duties of checking in borrowed books, and checking out new ones. I helped a gentleman research some old magazine articles in the archives department and assisted an elderly woman with locating a book about break dancing techniques. I was hoping she was checking it out for her grandson. Considering she walked with a cane, I couldn't see her spinning in spastic circles on the floor without breaking a hip, or dislocating every bone in her tiny, frail body.

At around ten o'clock, I looked up and saw a group of people standing at the front counter. One was a slim black woman in her twenties with three small children in tow, and the other adult was a heavyset white woman in the same age bracket, who had a piercing through her eyebrow and was wearing a tank top three sizes too small for her.

By the collection of tattoos she sported, I felt sure her decision to wear the tank top was prompted by her desire to show off the butterfly tat above her ample breast, and the nearly life-sized inked eagle across the top of her back. I was tempted to judge the heavier gal by her looks, but was glad I chose not to. As it turned out, she couldn't have been a nicer or more thoughtful young woman.

"May I help you ladies?" I asked.

"Yes, please," the pretty black lady replied. "I was wondering if I could get a library card."

"Of course! We just happen to have one," I said as I opened a box sitting on the counter to reveal dozens of blank cards.

I began signing the young woman up for her library card, after complimenting her on her adorable and well-behaved children. Her name was Abigail Allen, but her friend, Coral, referred to her as Abbie. In conversing politely with her I discovered that her twenty-seven year old husband, Blake, had joined the Marine Corp three years prior and was currently deployed overseas, stationed at Camp Leatherneck in Helmand, Afghanistan. Blake was a Lance Corporal E-3, she explained.

She went on to tell me he was based out of Camp Lejeune in North Carolina, but since he was planning to get out of the service as soon as he completed his four-year stint, and the Allens wanted to raise their family in the Midwest, she was living in Rockdale to establish their home here. Apparently, what little family they had lived in Kansas and Missouri, and the cost of living here was more affordable for them on her husband's salary than on the East Coast. All four of the couple's parents had died at a young age, and between them they had two aunts, one uncle, and several cousins in the area.

After I finished assigning Abbie her library card, she wandered off to the children's section, presumably to pick out some books to read to her kids. Coral, with the impressive ink collection, stayed behind to continue conversing with me. She told me she and Abbie had been best buds since grade school and that she was very worried about her friend.

"How come?" I asked. "Is she ill?"

"No, not physically, at least. But I've never seen her so depressed and stressed out. She's making herself sick with worry, and has lost ten pounds in the last few months. I'd love to lose weight without even trying, but as you can see, she can't afford to lose much more. She's already too thin."

"Is it because of her husband being deployed?"

"Well, there's that, of course. She and the kids will particularly be missing him over the holidays. But also, she is doing everything she can within their tight budget to keep afloat. She can't afford childcare in order to hold down a job," Coral said.

"I'm sure with three small children, she'd barely break even," I agreed.

"That's it exactly. She's afraid of losing their home and her and the kids being forced to live in her old car. Me and my two kids are living in a one-bedroom apartment, so there's no way I could take them in, long-term anyway."

"The poor thing," I said before Coral continued.

"But, she's especially depressed about the fact she won't be able to afford a decent Christmas supper, a tree to decorate, or even any presents for Seth, Hailey, and little Dax. I think they have macaroni and cheese for supper nearly every night, because it's cheap and they can buy it in bulk at Costco. She's living on a shoestring stretched so tight it's apt to snap at any moment. I'd help her if I could, but I'm barely able to afford my own bills."

"How about Blake's salary?" I asked.

"Well, with only having three years in the Marine Corps, he doesn't make enough to support all five of them. He was unemployed when he was sent on a tour to

Afghanistan and they were already in debt at the time," Coral explained. "And there's no job waiting for him to return to when he gets home either."

"Isn't she getting any kind of government assistance?"

"Yes, but unfortunately, not nearly enough."

"I've got an idea, but I'll have to discuss it with my husband first," I told Coral. She looked perplexed, but hopeful, at my comment. "Give me your phone number and I'll be in touch with you."

After Coral left the counter to join her friend, Abbie, and the kids, my mind began to spin off in many different directions, which is scary when you are already as scatter-brained as I sometimes am. I didn't know what I was going to do yet, but I knew I had to do something to brighten this family's holidays, or I wouldn't be able to enjoy the Christmas season myself

Evening found me warming up some leftover barbecued beans in the new microwave/convection oven Stone had installed for me during the afternoon. I'm pretty sure he stopped by Home Depot and purchased $500 worth of new tools to install a $400 appliance, but I was in no position to complain.

I had called my daughter earlier in the day to arrange a family meeting at the inn that evening. I wanted to discuss an idea with everyone while we dined on grilled tuna steaks, sweet potatoes, and the barbecued beans warming up in the new oven. Wyatt had already made plans to join us for supper, so the five of us would eat in the kitchen while our guests, the Harringtons, would enjoy their meal in the formal dining room.

Wendy, who worked as the assistant county coroner, would drive to the inn straight from work, and her boyfriend, Andy Van Patten, who also happened to be Stone's nephew, would commute from the ranch they lived on outside Atchison, Kansas. Like his Uncle Stone,

Andy had relocated to Rockdale from the East Coast.

Detective Johnston was already in the garage admiring Stone's brand new circular saw, which I was quite certain was not necessary to install the microwave/convection oven. However, I could fully understand his compulsion to buy a gift for himself as a reward for so patiently accepting the responsibility of replacing the appliance I had destroyed due to my complete inattention to what I was doing. Truthfully, he should already own every single power tool on the market for fixing all the things I'd broken during our short marriage.

A few minutes later, I heard Wendy come in through the back door of the inn. When she walked into the kitchen, I asked her about Andy's whereabouts.

"He's out in the maintenance shed with the guys. He wanted to see Stone's new edger."

"His new edger? Really?" I asked. I knew an edger played no part in installing a kitchen appliance, but it was beginning to dawn on me why Stone never seemed at all upset about having to fix or replace something I'd mangled, shattered, or blown up. In fact, I had thought he'd acted almost too cheerful when he grabbed the fire extinguisher to put out the incinerated potato. At that moment, I realized there were probably already visions of power tools and lawn equipment dancing in his head while he was extinguishing the fire.

"Can I help with anything?" Wendy asked, while I kept an eagle eye on the beans in the microwave. I knew Stone's patience might run out if he had to replace the microwave oven two days in a row. On the other hand, he might welcome the opportunity to return to Home Depot. There might be a shiny new fifty-four-inch, zero-turn John Deere mower he was hankering for.

After Stone said grace, and everyone filled their plates, I told them all about Abigail Allen and her family, and the current situation they were dealing with. Everyone at the table expressed a desire to help them out in some way.

"I was thinking about our family adopting their family for the holidays," I said. Stone, Wendy, and Andy all nodded their heads in agreement.

"That sounds intriguing. I'd like to be a part of that too," the detective said.

"We consider you part of the family, Wyatt. So, of course, we want you and Veronica to be involved."

"What did you have in mind?" Stone's nephew asked.

"Well, Andy, I thought maybe we could take up a collection for them. I think this community would reach out and be willing to help a local family that was struggling to make ends meet. We could ask for gifts for the children, and household goods such as clothes soap, paper towels, tin-foil and things such as that, to help Abbie stretch her own money further. Those things add up and take a large bite out of a budget."

"How about food too?" Wendy asked. "We can collect nonperishable items such as soup, peanut butter, cereal, and canned meats. The list of things they could use is practically endless. We don't want them to be in dire straits again already the day after Christmas."

"That's a marvelous idea!" I replied. "Anybody else have any suggestions?"

Wyatt nodded and said, "I can put up a big trash container-type barrel in the city services building. We already have a bin in the storeroom that would work perfectly. With the fire department, police department, and city offices all sharing the building, we're sure to collect a lot of items for the Allen family."

"And I can do the same thing at the library," I said. "Maybe I can put a little article in the *Rockdale Gazette* asking people to stop by one location or the other to donate an item or two, which will help a local family in need. We won't want to identify the family by name, of course. We don't want to take a chance of humiliating or embarrassing them. It's difficult enough for some people to accept charity as it is."

"How about seeing if we can also put a collection container in the entrance foyer at Pete's Pantry?" Andy asked. "I'm sure a lot of people wouldn't hesitate to drop a newly purchased grocery or household item in it as they exited the grocery store."

"I'm not sure about asking Pete's Pantry," I said. "I'm not the store manager, Edward's, favorite person after I accidentally caused a few little mishaps—"

"—big hairy messes," Wendy cut in.

"Well, okay, an entire display's worth of broken spaghetti sauce jars did make for a pretty substantial clean-up job. But accidents happen, and Edward really wasn't very understanding about it. I even offered to pay for all the broken jars. He really should be more of a people person to hold that position there, I think."

"Oh yeah," Andy said with a laugh. "I remember Wendy telling me about that now. Maybe someone else should approach him with the request, Lexie. He probably doesn't feel like he owes you any favors."

"I'll do it," Wyatt volunteered. "I've known Edward for years, and I've no doubt he'll let us put a collection container in the store. He's really not a bad guy. But I probably shouldn't tell him it was all your idea, Lexie. You may have tried his patience a little too much."

"No, I wouldn't recommend telling him you even know me," I replied. "And another idea I had is to treat the family to Christmas dinner here at the inn. We might even arrange to have a Santa Claus on hand to pass out gifts to Seth, Hailey, Dax, and even Abbie."

"I hope you're not planning on preparing the dinner all by yourself. I don't think serving them an undercooked, bacteria-ridden turkey is going to make their holidays any merrier," Wendy said. "You've been known to poison dinner guests before, you know."

I briefly wondered what I'd ever done to my daughter to make her so sarcastic and hostile. Okay, she might have inherited the sarcasm trait from me, but I was certainly not downright rude to my elders the way she was on occasion. I thought it might be fortunate for her that she was too old now to put in a foster home. God knows I'd threatened to put her up for adoption numerous times during her childhood, and once or twice, I might have actually done it if I'd been able to find anyone who wanted a back-talking, temper-tantrum-throwing brat, with a head that was harder than a bowling ball. Lucky for her, I couldn't pay anyone enough to take her off my hands.

"No, Wendy," I replied. "I was planning on having you prepare all the food while I whiled away the hours on the back porch with a canteen full of coffee. Have I reminded you lately how many hours of excruciatingly painful labor I suffered through just to give you life? Twenty-four long hours I spent trying to pass something that felt like a twelve pound kidney stone."

"No, you haven't reminded me of that since last week, Mom, and then it was only eighteen hours of *excruciatingly painful labor* trying to pass something that felt like a ten pound bag of potatoes. Your story gets more dramatic with every telling."

"Whatever," I said with a smile. "The point is you owe me—big time!"

"Okay, Mom, you know I'd love to help out, and I bet Veronica would too, since she and Wyatt will be sharing Christmas dinner with us."

Veronica was the daughter of the late Horatio Prescott III, who was murdered in our nicest suite at the inn on the opening night of the Alexandria Inn. Following the investigation into her father's death, which I played a major role in I might add, Veronica moved back home to Rockdale from where she'd been living in Salt Lake City. She took over ownership of Horatio's historic Italianate Mansion, which, with my advice, she'd turned into a lodging facility like ours. I often recommended Victoria's *Little Italy Inn* to people when ours was filled to capacity.

After Veronica returned to Rockdale, she and Wyatt, who were high school classmates in the 1990's, had reconnected and were now in a long-term relationship. He still owned an apartment in town, but I'm pretty sure he spent most of his evenings at Veronica's.

Veronica was an accomplished cook, like anyone involved with Wyatt would need to be, and I'm sure between Wendy and her, there would be little chance of me being responsible for anything more challenging than opening a can of cranberry sauce. If I didn't cut my finger with the lid and bleed all over the sauce, I could surely accomplish the task without causing a dining disaster. I'd proven in the past that even heating up dinner rolls was occasionally beyond my level of cooking competency.

"I just had another idea," I said. "Abbie's friend, Coral, who told me about the Allen family's plight, also mentioned that she was a single mother of two, and barely able to stay afloat herself. I think we should include them in our Christmas dinner and celebration, as well. As they say, the more the merrier. And if we're planning to get someone to impersonate Santa Claus anyway, why not brighten the holidays for another family if we can? I'm sure we'll have enough donated toys to go around, even if I have to purchase them myself."

Stone pretended to be insulted when we all agreed he'd be the perfect person to play Santa with his light silver - nearly white - hair, and slightly protruding belly. But he readily agreed and I could tell he was anxiously anticipating the experience. Once we had all our plans in place, we finished eating our supper and retired to the parlor for cherry cobbler and after-supper coffee. I could hardly wait to set those plans into motion.

CHAPTER 3

A few days later, all three of the collection bin sites were set up and donations were pouring in. Wendy had stopped at a Kinkos in St. Joseph, where she worked in the coroner's lab, and had three professional-looking signs created. The signs simply read *Please contribute a toy, household product, or nonperishable food item to help a local military family in need this holiday season as the father is deployed overseas.* Apparently that was all it took to open the hearts of the citizens of Rockdale, who, no doubt, hoped the community would stand behind them as willingly, should they ever find themselves in need of assistance.

As the collection bins filled up over the next several weeks, we began storing the toys at City Hall, where Wyatt knew there was a large unused storeroom available. We had decided early on to deliver the food and household products to the Allen family as they came in so they wouldn't have to struggle throughout November, and most of December, as well.

When I had spoken to Abigail's friend, Coral, she had been thrilled with our plan to adopt the Allen family for the holidays. She had given me Abbie's phone number, and I had extended an invitation for her family to join ours for a Christmas supper and celebration on Christmas Day, as well. Coral had only a few distant relatives in the area, and no plans for Christmas Day, so accepted the invitation readily, and with much enthusiasm.

I then called Abigail Allen and explained to her I was the acting head librarian at the local library, which she'd met the previous day, and I had spoken with her friend, Coral, about their current situation. She sounded somewhat dubious at first, probably confused at why I was reaching out to her. I went on to explain that my family felt indebted to her and her husband for his service to our country and wanted to adopt her family for the holidays as a token of our appreciation. It was our way of giving back, I explained to her.

"My family would like to invite you and your children to spend Christmas Day with us at the inn, along with your friend, Coral, and her family. After a Christmas feast, Santa Claus will arrive and hand out gifts to all the children, and then we will have a short prayer and candle-lighting session to commemorate the reason for the season," I told her.

"Oh my gosh! I am just so astonished by all this,' Abbie replied. "I can't tell you how appreciative I am for what you are offering my family. I've been so worried about how my kids will feel at Christmas with their father away, no decorated tree, and little in the way of presents."

Her response spurred an idea in my head. My impulsive nature made me want to do even more for the Allen family then we'd already discussed. "We will be bringing over a Christmas tree, and some ornaments for you all to enjoy in your own home, and of course, there will be a large tree at the inn on Christmas Day. We'll also put a few of the donated toys under your tree for the kids to find when they wake up Christmas morning."

I could hear the lilt in her voice as the magnitude of what we had in mind to do for her and her kids dawned on her. Her happiness soon turned to tears of joy. She was sniffling as she spoke. "How will we ever be able to repay you for your kindness?"

"Your husband fighting to preserve our freedom, and you making sacrifices at home while he serves as a Marine, is all the payment we could ask for, Abigail. It is an honor and a privilege for my family to help yours."

"Wow! I'm absolutely stunned! Oh, and please call me Abbie."

"Okay, Abbie it is. We are also collecting household and food items, which we will be bringing over about once a week as they are received. Do you have a place to stockpile them? Hopefully they will help with your budget for months to come."

"Yes, we have a nearly empty pantry and a huge storage area in the basement. It's an older home and there is plenty of space in it," she replied. "Oh my gosh! I can't believe this! I am so overwhelmed by your family's generosity that I can hardly speak. Thank you so much, Ms. Starr!"

"Call me Lexie, honey, and it's not just my family doing this. It is the generosity of the entire community; neighbors who want to reach out to your family this holiday season, and show their appreciation for your husband's service to our country."

When I hung up the phone a short while later, I was overcome with a feeling of great joy. I realized then that it truly *was* better to give than to receive.

It soon became clear to all of us that there was going to be a far greater number of toys donated than Abbie and Coral's children could ever need or play with. In the first week alone, we collected nine remote control trucks, fourteen Lalaloopsy dolls, and multiple duplicated less expensive toys. A few people were even donating new, and some used but in perfect condition, video games for electronic gaming devices that their own children probably no longer played with.

This sparked two decisions. As a gift to the children from the Alexandria Inn, we would give both families an Xbox 360 and pick out a number of appropriate games for each child from the donated selection. Some of the games were obviously designed for older children, or even adults, so we would weed those out in our selection process. These video games would keep the kids content for hours on end, particularly when the weather was not conducive for playing outdoors.

For Abigail and Coral, we'd purchase a couple of Kindles or Nooks to give to them so they could download books to read to their children or for themselves. With so many free downloads available, it would be cheap entertainment for the entire family. I had purchased myself a Kindle last Christmas, and I spent a lot of time reading books on it while lazing around on slow days.

My second decision was to donate all the excess donated toys to the nearest chapter of the Toys for Tots program, sponsored by the United States Marine Corps. I knew there was a chapter in Leavenworth, Kansas, which wasn't too far from Rockdale. With Fort Leavenworth located there, I figured it would benefit some military families, as well as provide Christmas gifts for other underprivileged children in the area.

I was so pleased with myself it was almost nauseating. I was mentally patting myself on the back for conceiving such a marvelous idea, and overjoyed with the results so far. Our plan was coming together seamlessly and could not be proceeding any smoother, or at least, not until Wyatt called me one morning several weeks later.

"Lexie?" I heard Wyatt's concerned voice over the phone.

"Yes. What's wrong?"

"Did you or Stone remove a bunch of the toys today from the storeroom?"

"No, neither of us has even been to City Hall in several days. Why do you ask? Are there some missing?"

"Yes, a lot of them," Wyatt replied. "All of the more expensive toys are missing, as well as every video game we've collected so far."

"Who in the world, other than any of us, would take them?" I asked.

"I don't know. When I locked up the storeroom last night they were all here, but when I came in here this morning a lot of them were missing."

"Isn't there normally a guard on duty? There's been one standing just inside the front revolving door nearly every time I've gone into the city services building. Where was he at the time?"

"Willie Cooper was on guard duty at the time, but he isn't always standing right at the front door. The guards get coffee breaks, restroom breaks, and at night they sometimes wander around the building, just to make sure nothing is amiss," Wyatt explained. "There's also a rear door to the building that is locked 24/7, but anyone can leave the building through that door. Willie checks that exit once in awhile too, and monitors the security camera system."

"Isn't Mr. Cooper the guy who founded that orphanage just north of town? I read an article in the *Gazette* about it not too long ago."

"Yes, that's him," Wyatt said. "Willie retired from the police department about five years ago, but recently took on the guard job to help support the orphanage, which is a bare-bones operation. He recently became an independent seller on eBay, buying and selling things to generate money for the orphanage."

"What a generous man," I said. "According to the article, he was a widow, and after his wife's death he'd dedicated his life to helping orphans find new homes and families. Mr. Cooper was orphaned at an early age and transferred from one foster home to another, never staying long at any of them. It was a tough childhood, the article read, and it made him want to help keep children from suffering the same fate."

"Yes, they just don't come any finer than Willie Cooper."

"Can we get a list of people Mr. Cooper remembers seeing in the building last night?" I asked.

"Sure, I know Willlie would be happy to help in any way he can. After all, his life revolves around helping children."

"Terrific! So, who all has access to a key to the storeroom?" I asked.

"Every department has a set of keys to the storeroom and various other rooms in the building. But since yesterday was Sunday, there were only a handful of people in the building during the evening. I was only here to bring over a bunch of toys from the collection bin at Pete's Pantry, including three more of those Lalaloopsy dolls. But those three dolls, and all the rest of them, were stolen along with a lot of other toys."

"What are we going to do, Wyatt? Are you going to fill out a police report? Will the department investigate the theft?" I had a sick feeling in my stomach. What kind of lowlife would steal Christmas toys from children whose entire holiday cheer depended on them? Someone who'd do something like that fell right between an axe-murderer and a pedophile in my opinion. They were certainly all in the same class of scum-of-the-earth individuals.

"Lexie," Wyatt said. "I will fill out a report, naturally, but I'm not sure how much attention this case will get. I'll see what I can do, but I'm not sure it will be enough. We probably should move the remaining toys to the inn and maybe store them in your basement there, just to make sure another theft like this one doesn't occur."

"Good idea. But what about the stolen toys, Wyatt? Shouldn't we try to recover them and find out who's responsible for the theft?"

"It would probably be a wasted effort. Besides, there will be plenty of additional toys donated. We still have three weeks until Christmas to collect more. And there are still some of the smaller toys left," he said, in an effort to boost my spirits.

"I just don't think the thief should get away with stealing toys right out of childrens' hands. We need to get our donation to the Leavenworth Toys for Tots center soon so they'll have them to distribute before Christmas. And, considering the total value of the donations, it is grand larceny, which, if I'm not mistaken, is still a felony."

"I know. I know. I wish I could do more. But I do have an idea I never thought I would suggest," Wyatt said with an audible sigh.

"What's that?"

"You've had a lot of luck investigating and tracking down murderers in the past. And although I didn't condone you risking your life the way you did on numerous occasions, I think your safety is pretty much guaranteed if you do a little investigating into this toy theft," he said with another, even louder, sigh. I could tell he was already regretting his suggestion, so I wanted to jump all over it before he changed his mind.

"Yes! Yes! I'll do it! I'd love to nail this royal asshole!" I nearly shouted in glee.

"Oh boy. Your enthusiasm has me worried already. Not to mention the fact that Stone is going to want my head on a platter when he hears I actually made this suggestion. I might want to rethink this decision, Lexie," Wyatt said. "I know how determined you are, and how reckless you can be when you are on a seek and destroy mission. I'm not sure in this situation how you can land yourself in major trouble, or worse, a life or death scenario, but if there's a way to do it, you will find it."

"I promise I'll be careful, Wyatt, and I won't do anything even remotely dangerous or risky in any way."

"Yeah, I've heard that a time or two before, so whether you like it or not, I also want you to try to promise to keep Stone and me aware of your actions and whereabouts at all times. Promise?" He asked.

"Really? At all times?" I asked. "Wyatt, you know I can't promise you that!"

"Okay, but will you at least try to keep us in the loop as much as possible?"

"Oh, all right, I'll try my best," I said, but not without a little hesitation. I tended to have the best luck when operating on my own. But I also tended to often find myself in deep doo-doo when I was evasive about where I was and what I was up to.

Well, I thought, deep doo-doo or not, here I go again!

Wendy stopped by the inn on her way back to the ranch after work that evening. She handed me a check for $240, which she'd received when she took up a collection for the Allen family at the coroner's lab. Nate, her boss and chief medical examiner for the county, had contributed $100 to the cause. Wendy said, "Nate is the most kind-hearted person I've ever met. That's why he is such a delight to work with.'

"Groovy," I replied without thinking. "That money will be useful to Abbie for paying utility bills, or something of that nature."

"Groovy?" Wendy said, with a touch of disbelief in her tone. "Whoa there Beach Boy! Welcome to the twenty-first century, Mom!"

"Sorry, old habits are hard to break," I said. "I meant to say *awesome*. You know, sometimes it's hard to trick old dogs."

"Oh, good Lord! The phrase is 'you can't teach an old dog new tricks.' If you're going to use old worn-out clichés, at least use them properly. But, hey, kudos on the 'awesome' thing. Jeez, Louise. As someone from your generation might say, I'm glad this nut *did* fall far from the tree."

"Huh?"

"Never mind," she said. "What was it you said you wanted to tell me when I spoke to you earlier on the phone?"

I told her about the theft of the toys, and also that Wyatt had suggested I take it upon myself to investigate the crime. I was very proud of this display of trust and confidence by the detective, who'd had to rescue me more than once, and I wanted to impress my normally skeptical daughter with the news.

"Is Wyatt frigging nuts?" She shouted, incredulously. "Has Wyatt even met you? Has he forgotten all the many times he, or someone else, has had to pull your tit out of the wringer in the past?"

"Wendy! Be nice!"

"I'm serious, Mom. Every single time you get involved in investigating a crime you end up with your own life in danger. How many times have you been in the emergency room in just the last two years because of your insistence on meddling in the police department's responsibilities? It's beyond me how you're even still among the living. I guess it's true that God protects children and fools."

"Those previous cases were murder cases, Wendy. This is just a little theft issue. Even Wyatt thought I'd be perfectly safe, and that a toy thief wouldn't be nearly as dangerous as a killer who has nothing to lose," I said. I didn't appreciate my own daughter implying that I was a fool. I may occasionally do something slightly foolish, but I was nobody's fool. "And, besides that, I assured him I'd try to keep him and Stone apprised of my actions and whereabouts."

"Gee, like you haven't made that same statement several times in the past, and still ended up with your foolish neck on the line!"

"Okay, enough with the 'fool' reference! You've made your point. But in each case there were circumstances that were beyond my control. Am I going to have to remind you again of what I went through bringing you, my disrespectful child, into the world?"

"No, please don't," she replied with a dramatic groan. "I don't like it one little bit, however, there's not much I can do if Wyatt actually asked you to get involved, that big nincompoop! But mark my words, nothing good can come of this, and that boneheaded cop is probably going to regret he made such an addlebrained decision. I love the goofball to death, but I can't believe he'd actually encourage you this way. I think he must have a doughnut lodged in his brainstem, or something."

"Okay, okay, you've made your point—again! Cut the poor guy some slack. He's as incensed as I am that some stupid schmuck would willingly rip the holiday spirit to shreds, and take toys right out of the hands of needy children. Talk about a grinch!"

"Well, that's the first thing you've said so far in this conversation that I agree with. Those Lalaloopsy dolls aren't cheap. At least the thief didn't make off with a bunch of Furbies," Wendy said.

"Furbies? What's that?"

"They are fluffy owl-like robots that can sleep, eat, dance and talk. They can even be taught new behaviors. I guess they are pretty amazing. The Furby is the hottest toy on the market this year, and they're very difficult to find. I heard all the area stores were sold out of them,"

Wendy explained. "So, naturally, they are on every kid's wish list."

"No wonder we haven't seen any of them in our collection bins. But, according to Wyatt, the container at City Hall is already filling up again. Probably the only reason it hasn't been stolen from its location at the reception desk is because it's in full view of the security guard. There's a guard there around the clock, even when the building is locked down."

"As much as I hate to ask, what is your first plan of action?" Wendy asked, with trepidation in her voice. The labored way she was all of a sudden breathing concerned me. If she were asthmatic, I'd have thought she was having an attack.

"Wyatt is getting me a list of people who were in the building last night, from Willie Cooper, the guard on duty at the time. After I get that list, I'll have to decide where to turn first, and who all I think I need to interrogate."

"Interrogate? Oh my God! I can already see the writing on the wall," my ungrateful child said before hanging up the phone on me.

CHAPTER 4

The Harringtons checked out early the next morning. They planned to eat breakfast on the road. I guess they just weren't in the mood for soggy toast, runny eggs, and burnt bacon. But they seemed very appreciative for all we'd done to make their stay pleasant, including chocolate mints on the pillows of their bed each night, and the cheesy potatoes I'd made for them to take to a family potluck dinner. I can't say for sure that the casserole was particularly tasty, but at least they didn't show up at the get-together empty-handed.

I was sitting on the back porch with my usual cup of coffee and reading the *Gazette* when Stone joined me.

"Hi, honey," I greeted him. "Can you believe there's not one word about the donated Christmas toys being stolen from City Hall in the paper this morning?"

"That is surprising, but maybe there was more sensational news to be covered yesterday. You know they only have one full-time reporter, who can't be everywhere at once," Stone said, in defense of the small town daily newspaper.

"Oh, sure. What was I thinking? Gladys Coleman had her bunion removed, and Bernard Hill is thinking about planting corn instead of wheat next spring. And, believe it or not, Agnus Murphy is visiting her sister in Jefferson City this weekend. What could be more newsworthy than that? The only thing in this silly rag that even resembles news is that the juvenile delinquents who had been shooting up the town with their pellet guns are still on the lam. Jeez. Make sure you lock all the doors tonight, Stone. There are dangerous criminals on the loose in town."

"I'm beginning to wonder why you even subscribe to the *Rockdale Gazette*, Lexie," Stone said. "You complain about its contents every morning.

"Well, it's because I enjoy reading it so much with my morning coffee."

"You are something else, sweetheart," he said with a laugh. "But, I have to tell you, I am in complete agreement with Wendy. The toys can be replaced, but you can't. We'll have way more than enough for Abbie and Coral's kids, and plenty left over to contribute to the Toys for Tots program in Leavenworth. Why not just let the matter drop and concentrate on your plans for our Christmas celebration here at the inn?"

"Stone, can't you understand that it's the principle of the matter? It's a cruel and thoughtless crime that I feel should not go unpunished. We need to make an example of this jerk who would stoop so low as to steal from children."

"All right. I can see this is really important to you. I'll help in any way I can, but I am not going to let you go to extremes over a case like this one. It's just not worth putting your well-being into jeopardy. So, as you told Wyatt you would, I want you to try to never do anything, or go anywhere, without telling me first. Okay?"

"Oh, okay. If at all possible, I'll let you know where I

am and what I'm doing," I replied. I hated being restricted this way, knowing it would hamper my movement and progress in solving the case. But, I have been known to be evasive about my plan of action on a number of occasions before, and I was not above doing it again. I wouldn't outright lie to either my husband, or the detective, but I might not spell out the entire truth in detail either. What they didn't know wouldn't hurt me.

Just as I was making a vow to Stone to be as transparent as possible, Wyatt Johnston walked out onto the back porch. He carried his own key to the inn and could let himself in at any time, day or night. There was no one we trusted more than the detective.

Wyatt had swung by the kitchen and grabbed a cup of coffee and an apple fritter off a platter on the table. He sat down in an empty chaise lounge, and said, "I got the list you requested from Willie. He could only recall five people being in the building Sunday night besides himself and me. Chief Smith stopped by to pick up a recharged battery for his police radio, but ended up spending over an hour in his office. Mayor Bradley Dunn was also in his office, finishing some paperwork he hadn't had time to get to earlier in the week. Sammy Saragusa, the volunteer fireman, was manning the fire station, which, as you know, is on the opposite end of the building from the police station. Other than that, there were just Detective Clint Travis, the rookie cop you met last month, and Detective Michael Russell, who were on night shift duty at the time.

I was a little disappointed at the list of suspects I had to work with. None of them seemed capable of such a crime, as they were all in very trustworthy and prominent positions within the structure of the city's public servant organizations.

"Was he certain they were the only people to enter the building all night?" I asked.

"Fairly certain, but said he couldn't guarantee it. He

left his post on several occasions; to use the bathroom, do a security sweep of the entire building, and to get a cup of coffee out of the machine in the break room. I can't believe he can get that nasty stuff down. You are the only other person I know who could drink such awful-tasting coffee."

I started to defend myself, but quickly realized the detective was probably correct in his opinion about my ability to drink even the nastiest of coffees. I could swallow almost anything, no matter how unsavory, in order to get a shot of caffeine to feed my addiction.

"Well, if this unlikely list of suspects is all I have to work with, I'll just have to accept it and figure out who I want to speak to first," I said.

"I am going to lay down some ground rules, Lexie," Wyatt told me. "Any conversation you have with any of these individuals is to be held in a public place, in view of other people, if not Stone or I, and never in a private setting. Agreed?"

"Yeah, all right. I'll do my best to comply with your rules."

"And you are not to attempt anything with any measure of risk whatsoever. And I mean nothing even remotely hazardous. This is not a murder case, and the outcome's not critical enough to warrant getting yourself injured, or worse. Understand?"

"He's right, Lexie," Stone cut in. "Try to remember it didn't even merit a mention in the paper this morning. Gladys Coleman's bunion garnered more press time than this toy theft issue. Let's try not to make a mountain out of a molehill, and possibly get yourself into a dangerous situation in the process."

"Okay, I understand your concerns, but I still feel it's important to pursue the case, at least a little," I said. I felt like an unruly child being chastised for my unpredictable and adventurous behavior. I was born with those traits and I was a little too old to change my nature overnight.

But I had no choice but to agree with Wyatt's demands. I'd even try my best to adhere to them. Unfortunately, in the past, my best had never been quite good enough.

"Have you ever met the mayor, Bradley Dunn?" I asked Stone later in the afternoon. "I've seen photos of him in the paper, and read articles about him, too. I also remember seeing him in the back of the room at the little ceremony they had when Chief Smith presented me with a Certificate of Appreciation last month. But he left before I could speak to him or introduce myself."

"I was able to speak to him briefly at the ceremony," Stone replied. "I've also seen him at the Friday night auction at the Bargain Barn on Willow Street several times. I think I spoke to him only once in passing at the auction barn, and that's about the extent of my interaction with him."

"Does he go to the weekly auction often?" I asked.

"Well, I've been to it three times, and he's been there each time, so I'd guess he was a regular attendee. Why do you ask, or do I even want to know?"

"I've decided to go to the auction tomorrow night. Would you like to go with me?" I asked.

"Sorry, dear, I can't. There's a Chamber of Commerce meeting at seven and I have to speak about a new law we want to lobby for, and as a member of the board of directors, it's important I show up for the meetings," he said. "Maybe we can go to the auction next week instead."

"That's eight days away. We don't have that much time. Can't I go to the auction by myself? After all, I am complying with Wyatt's ground rules. I'm giving you fair notice where I'll be, and if I get a chance to speak to the mayor, it will be in a public setting where I'm surrounded by a lot of other people," I reasoned.

"I hope I don't live to regret this, but all right, you can go to the auction alone. Remember that it's very important we stay on good terms with the mayor, and every one else on your suspect list. Please don't imply that you think he stole those toys if you get an opportunity to talk to him."

"All right," I said, but not without acting a little put out at being told what to do at fifty-years old. A person was never too old to pout a bit when the situation called for it.

"I hope you realize that I know you're an adult and I can't tell you what to do. I'm only concerned about your welfare. You are the love of my life and I don't know what I'd do without you. Do you understand my concern?" Stone tempered his comments with a tender kiss on my forehead, and a soft stroking of my arm. I marveled again at how lucky I was to have landed this gentle, loving man as my husband, even though at times I could do without the over-protectiveness he exhibited.

"Of course I do, and I love you for it, Stone. I'll be discreet, and I'll take no chances whatsoever. I will just bring up the subject of the toy theft and feel him out on the subject. I'm certainly not going to accuse the mayor of stealing toys, for goodness sakes! But maybe he'll have some insight on the theft of the toys, or have some idea who might have been responsible for it."

"Do me one favor, honey. Don't tell Wyatt or Wendy that I agreed to your decision to try to approach the mayor at the auction tomorrow night. I don't need either one of them questioning my sanity."

"I had absolutely no intention of telling either one of them. They both already made it clear what they think about my state of mind.

When I walked into the smoke-filled auction barn the following evening, I looked around the room for a portly gentleman with less than a handful of hairs strategically combed across his head in a pitiful attempt to look like he wasn't only fourteen plucks short of being completely bald.

I spotted him almost immediately. He was surrounded by a swarm of men who were vying for his attention, and I could hear his bellowing laugh clear across the room when someone tickled his funny bone. I watched him reach up and pat down his few remaining hairs, apparently to prevent his secret of being nearly bald from getting let out of the bag.

I wasn't planning on bidding on anything, but I wanted to look like I had a reason to be there, so I signed up at the counter and was given a wooden placard with the number sixty painted on it.

I then headed to the concession stand to purchase a large cup of coffee. After one sip of the strong brew, I decided the city hall's vending machine couldn't possibly produce coffee that tasted any worse than the cup I'd just paid three bucks for. But that, of course, didn't prevent me from planning to drain the cup and possibly return for a refill.

If at all possible, I wanted to land a seat right next to the mayor. I walked over and with my back to the throng of people enveloping him, I pretended to be engrossed in a text message on my phone. I was on high alert, waiting for him to make a step toward the metal bleachers, which were like those you'd find in a junior high school gymnasium.

When at last he headed in that direction, I dashed toward him, nearly knocking three people over in the process. In my haste, I spilt about a quarter cup of the crappy coffee on the back of an elderly man's overalls, but he seemed oblivious to it, so I didn't stop to apologize. However, I did rue the loss of about seventy-five cents worth of the awful tasting, but caffeine-infused, beverage. Maybe Wyatt was right. I had no boundaries when it came to drinking coffee.

When I realized that I wasn't going to beat a tall, slim gentleman coming from the opposite direction, to the only empty seat next to Bradley Dunn, I pointed to the floor directly behind the lanky fellow, and hollered, "Look out!"

When the man stopped abruptly, and turned around in alarm, I practically flung myself into the seat he'd been about to sit down on. The bewildered gentleman looked back toward me with a questioning expression, and I said, "Oh, I'm sorry. I thought I saw a big wad of gum on the floor and I didn't want you to accidentally step on it and get it all over your shoes. It must have just been one of those floaters I've been prone to ever since my botched retinal surgery."

The man just shrugged, and looked at me like he'd just come in contact with an escapee from an insane asylum. He turned around and found himself a seat three rows back on the opposite side of the bleachers. I felt a little embarrassed, but I got over it quickly when I reminded myself I'd been successful in getting a seat right next to the mayor. In my somewhat crazed state of mind, it was akin to getting an audience with the Pope.

I didn't want to seem too obvious or anxious to speak to Mr. Dunn, so I sat quietly while the auctioneer began speaking in that rapid-fire manner that always amazed me. When I heard a mosquito flying by my ear, I swatted at it and unintentionally bid fifteen bucks on an old accordion that looked like it had been shipped to America on the Mayflower. Luckily, another woman who looked nearly as old as the accordion outbid me.

After several more items had been auctioned off, there was a pause in the action as the auctioneer's assistant went to retrieve the next item on his list.

I took this opportunity to turn to the mayor, and ask, "Aren't you Mr. Dunn, the mayor of Rockdale?"

"Yes, ma'am," he replied, without even turning to acknowledge me with even a quick glance in my direction. A flitting gnat would have received more attention than I did.

"Did you happen to hear about the theft of some very expensive toys from the storeroom at City Hall, which had been donated to benefit underprivileged children?"

"Yeah, I heard something about that," he replied, with a total lack of interest.

"I'm the person who conceived the idea for the appeal to the public for toys and other helpful items for a struggling family in our community. Do you have any idea who could have done such an awful thing as to steal some of these donated items? I know you were in the building that evening, and I wondered if you happened to see anything unusual, or see anyone suspicious enter or leave the building, possibly with a large box of toys," I spoke earnestly.

"No, sorry. I've been too busy with a lot more important things to dwell on then the loss of some silly toys. An issue like that, of such low caliber, would have been the last thing on my mind Sunday night. I really can't be bothered with such trivial matters when I have an entire town to look after."

He turned away from me, as if to signal my allotted thirty seconds of his precious time were up. His nonchalant dismissal of the theft and me infuriated me. Who did he think he was? Maybe he thought he really was as important as the Pope, and his time was beyond valuable.

This was Rockdale, where the streets were rolled up at seven, and the three stoplights in town began blinking red at that same time. How could this pompous ass show such little regard for the welfare of local citizens, and the happiness of helpless children? I knew Stone wanted to stay on the good side of all the people involved with the city government, but I couldn't suppress my anger with Mayor Bradley Dunn's callous attitude, and his condescending treatment of a family in his jurisdiction.

"So you think that our local families who are in need are of no importance, and their financial difficulties are not worth your time or effort? Are you only concerned with your country-club buddies, and who you consider to be the pillars of society? I assume you think people of a lesser social status are too far beneath you to care about?" I asked, practically snarling at the mayor, who was staring at me in total disbelief.

"Lady, I'm through talking with you about the loss of a few toys. I'm not on the clock right now and I'm here to enjoy the auction, not deal with your petty little problems," Mayor Dunn said, with an evil glint in his eyes.

I knew I was over-reacting, and my arms were flailing about in my angst, but I despised people like Bradley Dunn who thought their you-know-what didn't stink. I tried to stop myself, I really, truly did. But, despite my best efforts, I blurted out, "Maybe the real reason you don't want to be bothered about the toy theft situation is because you had something to do with it!"

"Sold for $300 to bidder number sixty!" I heard the auctioneer's voice ring out. I froze in my tracks, just as I was about to level even more outrageous thinly veiled accusations at the mayor. Did the auctioneer just say bidder number sixty? Why did that number sound familiar? I looked down at my bidding placard in horror. Before it had time to register that the auctioneer had mistaken my gestures as a winning bid, he had moved on to another item.

I wanted to yell out that I hadn't meant to bid on the previous item, but realized I would look totally ridiculous. I'd probably already attracted enough attention by screaming at one of the most influential people in Rockdale. Besides, it was my fault, not the auctioneer's. I knew better than to make any sudden moves during a sale of this nature, because any given nod, twitch, or tic, could be mistaken as a desire to increase the bid on an item being auctioned off.

While I was ruminating about what I had just

committed to paying $300 for, the mayor had stood up and walked away from his seat, disappearing from sight within seconds. I scanned the room, but didn't see him anywhere. Not that it mattered. I couldn't imagine he had any intention of saying another word to me.

I could see no point in staying any longer. Bradley Dunn had just moved to the top of my suspect list. I knew the mayor and his wife had several small children and the salary of a small town mayor was minimal at best. Despite his highfaluting attitude, he might be struggling to keep up appearances amongst his peers. There had to be some reason, I thought, for his refusal to discuss the theft of the toys.

As I sat there in somewhat of a stupor, I was curious about what I was going to have to explain purchasing to Stone. Hopefully, it was something a little more useful than an ancient musical instrument I had no clue how to play.

When I stepped up to the counter to collect my 'prize,' the lady at the register looked at the computer screen, and said, "Oh, I was wondering who had bid on the *Reflections of a Shattered Mind* painting. I was beginning to think no one would. I was a little surprised at the hefty starting price for the thing, though. No offense."

As I wrote out a check for $300, and waited for another young gal to go and collect the painting from the back room, I thought maybe I'd lucked out. It would be easy to attribute my purchase to wanting to hang the, no doubt, fabulous, painting somewhere in the inn. The title of the artwork concerned me a bit, but it was common for artists to name their pieces in abstract terms. The lady's "no offense' remark had me a little worried too, as did the fact that no one bid against me for the honor of owning this pricey piece of art.

When the clerk returned to the counter with the most hideous so-called painting I'd ever seen, I almost swallowed my tongue in what felt like a small involuntary seizure. It wasn't only a colossal waste of oil-based paint, it was ungodly large, as well. I wanted to ask if an inebriated elephant had painted it with its trunk, hoping there was some logical reason it was nothing but a blob of different colors slapped haphazardly across the canvas. Surely, the artist had been high on LSD, or something of that nature, at the time he or she created this conglomeration that could have represented anything from an Asian lady on a bicycle to Pocahontas on a horse. I couldn't tell if it was a landscape, a still life, a portrait, or what, but I *could* tell it wasn't worth what I'd just paid for it.

I'll admit there were a lot of paintings, many of them crafted by well-known artists, that I just didn't *get.* While viewing them in art galleries, I often thought I could paint something just as worthy without a second of training, or a grain of artistic talent. Then, to cover for my inadequacy, I would simply describe my masterpiece as an abstract, which to me represented any painting that had no rhyme or reason to it, and could be created by any half-wit with a brush in their hand.

Maybe if I had studied the arts in college, I'd have more appreciation for this genre of artwork. Instead, I'd spent that time concentrating on perfecting my flirting skills in order to catch the eye of Chester Starr, the power forward on the university's basketball team, who would later become my first husband.

I had half a mind to stop at the first dumpster I saw and ditch the painting, which was not designed to be transported in a Volkswagen Bug. Fortunately, or in retrospect, regrettably, the car was a convertible. It was no more than forty degrees outside, and I had the top down so the painting could stand up on the back seat, and didn't have to be folded up to fit in my car, as if there were any way to make the damn thing less attractive.

People were staring at me and laughing at the fact I was obviously uncomfortably cold, and incredibly stupid. One guy even took a video with his cell phone, and no doubt immediately posted it on YouTube. I'd probably go viral by morning.

I had written the check for the monstrosity from my own account, so no one would be the wiser if I trashed the thing. It wouldn't be the first time I'd thrown perfectly good money into the wind, but the cheapskate in me wouldn't let me discard the worthless piece of crap that I had just squandered $300 on.

When I arrived back at the inn, I walked into the kitchen and leaned the painting up against the pantry door. Stone's meeting had been slated for six o'clock so I wasn't surprised to find him home already. He greeted me and glanced up from his iPad momentarily, before he resumed doing whatever he'd been doing when I walked into the room. Just when I thought he wasn't even going to make a comment, he said, "So, tell me, Lexie, what are you planning to do with that butt-ugly thing?"

While I explained, as briefly and vaguely as I could, why I was in the possession of the *butt-ugly thing*, Stone listened with a grim expression on his face. I went into as little detail as possible about my conversation with Bradley Dunn. However, knowing me as well as he did, he seemed to read between the lines and grasp the gist of it, and didn't look too pleased with my explanation. I sensed that I had a long sleepless night in my near future. Stone surprised me though, as he often did, by not mentioning another word about it as we prepared for bed.

I was not overjoyed to hear Detective Johnston and Wendy chatting with Stone at the kitchen table when I went downstairs the next morning. They were all chuckling and making disparaging remarks about the

Reflections of a Shattered Mind painting that was still propped up against the pantry door. Before I walked into the kitchen, I heard my daughter speaking with a great deal of sarcasm in her tone.

"I wonder whose shattered mind they were referring to, the artist or the buyer's? It should have been named *Reflections of a Wasted Canvas*."

I heard Wyatt laugh and reply, "Or how about Reflections of Three Hundred Bucks Down the Toilet?"

When I walked around the corner, the laughter stopped abruptly, and all three of them sat there with stupid grins as they tried to suppress their laughter. I wanted to slap the smirks right off their faces. "Wyatt, I swear that Danish you're devouring is the last pastry that's ever going to cross your lips in this house if you don't start treating me with a little more respect."

"Sorry, Lexie," he said, with a guffaw that slipped out despite his efforts to contain it. "I apologize for laughing at your expense. Seriously, that painting you bought is really not all that bad. I can see it hanging in the parlor for all your guests to admire."

With that last remark, all three of them lost it. I thought for a minute that I was going to have to pick Stone up off the floor and perform the Heimlich maneuver on Wyatt, because they were laughing so uncontrollably. For a moment, I even thought it would serve the detective right to get an apple crisp lodged in his windpipe. I poured myself a cup of coffee and walked out of the room to retreat to the back porch.

"You ungrateful pigs!" I said as I left the room. Not that any of them heard me over their incessant giggling.

It was just a few minutes later that the three of them joined me on the back porch, they apologized, but not without looking smug and highly amused as they did so. Once the conversation turned to the amount of donations flooding in, I asked the detective if he'd heard anything new about the *heist*, as I'd decided to refer to the incident. After all, the mayor had belittled the atrocious crime to such a degree, you'd think an old man had been caught red-handed taking a grape to taste-test at the supermarket before wasting several bucks on a full bag of them.

It might not be important to Bradley Dunn, but it was very important to me, and a lot of children in the county who might go without presents at Christmas if not for the generosity of others, and admirable programs like Toys for Tots.

Wyatt told me he'd spoken to the rookie cop, Detective Clint Travis, a cop I was familiar with, about what he remembered about Sunday night when he and his partner, Detective Michael Russell, were on duty at the police station.

"What did he say?" I asked.

"Travis said he and Russell had spent a couple of hours in the station, doing paperwork, because it was a slow night out on patrol. Being a Sunday night, there were very few people out and about and literally no calls coming into the dispatcher, which was the duty Russell was usually assigned to, and the one he was performing that night."

"Did they see anyone suspicious in the building that evening?" I asked.

"No, but Detective Travis did tell me that it was possible someone had come in undetected by the security guard. He claims there was no one on duty at the security desk when he left at the end of his shift. He assumed Willie Cooper was on break or using the restroom, and thought nothing more about it. But, as Travis indicated, someone could have entered the building at that time, gone to the storeroom to pilfer the toys, and then exited out the rear door. The rear door is always locked from the inside, so you can leave the building through it, but can't enter it unless someone inside opens it for you."

"Aren't there security cameras inside the building?" Stone asked. "Could the thief possible have been caught on tape?"

"If the cameras had been functioning, yes, but they were down and scheduled for repair at the time," Wyatt said. "It was a case of ill timing where the toy theft is concerned."

"Maybe it wasn't a coincidence at all," I said. "Maybe whoever stole the toys had something to do with the fact they weren't working Sunday night, or at least were aware of the fact they were off at the time."

"That's a thought," Wyatt said. "I never did hear exactly why or how they were malfunctioning. But with Willie away from his post on several occasions, anyone could have entered the building, considering the fact that the front revolving door wasn't locked. They could have stood outside and watched through the glass, waiting for Willie to abandon the security desk, and then snuck in at that time, snatched the toys, and exited out the rear door, which was located just a few feet from the storeroom where the toys were being stored. That means, of course, that our field of suspects is practically endless."

"There is one thing that Clint Travis said that seemed odd. He told me he walked up to Chief Smith's office to ask him about getting a day or two off around Christmas so he can spend some time with his four kids. As I told you in early November, Clint's been going through a brutal divorce, and fighting for joint custody of his children."

"Sure, I remember you telling us his wife was having an affair with his former best friend, who just happened to be a lawyer who handled divorce cases and had an in with most of the judges. As I recall you saying, when it came to the divorce settlement, Travis pretty much figured he was guaranteed to take it in the shorts," I said.

"Yeah, poor guy. His gut feeling has turned out to be

pretty spot-on so far," Wyatt said. "But, as I was saying, when Clint got to the chief's office, the door was closed, and he heard Smith talking to someone. He couldn't tell if the chief was talking on the phone or to someone meeting with him in his office, because he couldn't hear any other voices, but he thought the other person could have been speaking too softly for their voice to be heard from out in the hallway. Clint thought Chief Smith might possibly have been on the phone with his wife when he heard the chief refer to the person he was conversing with as 'darling.' But he then referred to her as Rachel, and Mrs. Smith is named Josephine."

"So, did Clint ever find out if this Rachel was speaking to the chief in person, or just over the phone?" I asked.

"No, he didn't want to get caught eavesdropping, and he had to clock out in a few minutes, so he just went back and joined Detective Russell in the main room where we each have a desk to work at when we fill out paperwork, which can be extensive," Wyatt explained. "Basically, what I'm saying is, that there could have been another person in the building who failed to check in at the front desk, which has been the standard protocol ever since nine-eleven, when nearly everyone cracked down on their security practices and regulations."

"I'm getting the feeling that even attempting to investigate the crime may turn out to be a complete waste of time and effort," I said, dejectedly. I wasn't one to give up easily, but I had to wonder if I was setting myself up for a time-consuming wild goose chase.

"Yes, it would!" Wyatt and Stone said in unison. They both looked hugely relieved at my remark. However, their smiles turned to grimaces soon after I made my next comment.

"I didn't say I was giving up my quest to catch this creep, guys, or at least not yet."

After listening to their chorus of groans, I continued.

"But time is running out, and if nothing turns up soon, I will just try to accept it and move on. So, tell me Wyatt, what do you know about the volunteer fireman, Sammy Saragusa, who was manning the fire station Sunday night?"

"I've talked to him a few times, but I don't know him well. He's divorced, like Clint Travis, but at least his was a mutual agreement between him and his ex-wife. He told me that they have several kids together."

"Who has custody of the children?" I asked.

"Sammy's ex-wife does. According to him, he is $3,000 behind in child support, though. Being in arrears doesn't seem to bother him much, but the amicable relationship they've had up until now is beginning to deteriorate. Our fire department is manned completely with volunteers, and his only paying job is part-time employment with a landscaping company, so he gets very few hours in during the winter months. He's trying to nail down a full-time position somewhere, or at least another part-time job to supplement his income, although he doesn't seem to be putting a lot of effort into his job search. He's a good guy, but laid back almost to a fault. I've heard he's a pro at fighting fires, though."

"Why doesn't Sammy move to a bigger city and get a full-time, paying fireman position with a fire department that isn't strictly voluntary?" Stone asked Wyatt.

"I guess he just loves Rockdale too much to leave here. A lot of folks who were born and raised in this small town refuse to live anywhere else. The quaintness and community spirit of Rockdale can get into your blood. I know it wouldn't be easy to pry me away from here, either," Wyatt replied.

"I can certainly understand that sentiment. I adore this town too, but I'd be stressed to the max if I were in his shoes. I don't believe I've ever met Sammy," I said.

"Probably not," Wyatt said. "As a woman, you'd probably remember if you'd met him before. He'd probably be a tough guy for women to forget. Have you ever seen that turquoise house on Sycamore Street that backs up to Boney's Garage?"

"How could I miss it? It practically glows in the dark," I replied, wondering what he meant by his remark about women having a hard time forgetting Mr. Saragusa.

"Well, that's the place Sammy is renting. I'd be surprised if his rent wasn't overdue, as well."

"Gosh, it seems like everyone is struggling right now. I know the economy is bad, but I didn't realize how many people were being so adversely affected by it. Well, I guess we can't help them all. I need to get going shortly. I want to go buy an artificial pre-lit Christmas tree and a few boxes of ornaments and take them over to the Allen house. Stone, can I borrow your truck?"

"Of course," Stone answered. "Would you like me to come along to load and unload the tree for you?"

"Thanks, but they don't tend to be all that heavy, and between Abbie and I, we'll manage all right. I might be gone awhile, because while I'm out I'm going to run by the vacuum repair shop to have them look at my new vacuum and hopefully repair it."

"Your $600 vacuum needs to be fixed already?" He asked. He hadn't stopped ribbing me about caving into the pressure applied by the door-to-door salesman who'd convinced me I not only wanted the incredible cleaning machine, I also desperately needed it. Like any salesman who comes to my door, he had immediately picked up the scent of a sucker in his midst, and quickly swooped in to close the deal. It was only after I closed the door behind him, holding my new over-priced vacuum, that I realized I'd been taken to the cleaners—no pun intended.

Just before I left the inn at ten o'clock, the house phone rang. When I saw the caller I.D. and realized the call was coming from the police station, I assumed it was Wyatt on the line.

"Ms. Starr?" The caller asked. I recognized the voice, but couldn't place it, until the man on the other end identified himself as Detective Clint Travis. He asked me if I remembered meeting him in early November, and I confirmed that I did. At our first meeting, Detective Travis had impressed me as being rude and insensitive, and somewhat of a jerk. But once I learned what was going on in his personal life, I understood his surly demeanor.

I asked Travis why he was calling and he informed me that he and Wyatt had discussed the theft of the toys from the storeroom. He said, "Wyatt told me you were looking into the matter, and I wanted to see if there was anything I could do to help."

"Thanks, Detective Travis. I'd appreciate it if you could just keep your eyes and ears open for anything, or anyone, that strikes you as suspicious."

"I'd be happy to," he replied.

"By the way, what do you know about Sammy Saragusa?"

"I've talked to the volunteer fireman on a number of occasions, and he seems like a very congenial and likable guy. I can't imagine him doing something so vile, but I don't really know him well. Hurting a child in any way is unthinkable to me. I would do anything for my kids, and I'm fighting tooth and nail just to get unsupervised visits with them right now."

"I'm so sorry for what you're going through, Detective. Wyatt told me a little about your situation."

"I doubt it is related to the missing toys, but I did see Saragusa pulling out of the parking lot that evening. About a half hour later, after my shift ended, I was walking to my car and saw him pulling back into the lot. He usually leaves the station at midnight, which was still two hours away. Now that I think about it, he probably just went out to get a bite to eat."

"Probably," I agreed. "But I'll keep it in mind as I speak to potential suspects."

"Well, keep me in mind, too, if you need help with anything," Detective Travis said before ending the call. My opinion of the detective raised another notch and I reminded myself not to judge people based on a first impression.

I had intended to question Detective Travis, who was in the building that Sunday night the toys were stolen, but I now concluded it would only be a waste of my time and effort. And time wasn't something I had a lot of to waste at this stage of the game.

"I poured myself a to-go cup of coffee, and headed out to go shopping. By noon I was pulling into Abbie's driveway with a pretty, but not overly large, artificial Christmas tree. It looked almost like a real pine tree, and the pre-strung lights twinkled like fireflies when plugged in. I felt sure it would light up the faces of Abbie, and her children, throughout the Christmas and New Year's holidays for years to come.

I had called Abbie beforehand to let her know I was on my way over to deliver the tree and the sack full of ornaments I'd purchased. When asked, she said they hadn't eaten lunch yet, so I arrived with three Happy Meals, two Big Macs, and five chocolate shakes to share with the Allens family.

All four of the Allen's couldn't have been any more appreciative, and the children were alive with excitement. They could hardly sit still long enough to eat due to their impatience to get started decorating their new tree. From chatting with Abbie, I found out that Seth was nine, Hailey was seven, and Dax had just turned four. I could tell they were being raised right, just by their politeness and good manners.

"Lexie, I have something to run by you," Abbie said. "My pantry is loaded, and my basement is nearly full. We have enough food and household items to last us a very long time now. I've received so much stuff already; I've even managed to fill Coral's cabinets up too. If it's all right with you and your family, I'd like to donate the remaining contributions to the local food bank. God knows they've helped us out plenty of times in the last few months."

"I think that's a marvelous idea, Abbie." I was more than happy to donate the extra items to the food bank that provided food supplies to whoever showed up on their doorstep in need. Often, when their supplies ran low, Stone, I, and many other Rockdale citizens, chipped in to help keep their shelves full. We felt it was a worthy charity to support.

There were far too many children in the world that went to bed hungry, and it pained me to think of even one child in our town not getting enough to eat. Children needed nourishment to grow strong and healthy, and to be able to concentrate on their studies at school. Without a good education, the circle of poverty would likely continue on to another generation. Every child deserved an opportunity to improve his or her lot in life. Lending a helping hand was the least we could do.

After I left the Allen house, I drove downtown and looked for a parking spot on Main Street. The sidewalks were bustling with people, even though snow flurries had begun to coat the pavement with a light dusting. Many of the pedestrians carried shopping bags, presumably trying to get all their gifts purchased before Christmas.

As it turned out, there was a car pulling away from the curb directly in front of the vacuum store as I pulled up. The repairman, who was also the owner of the store, looked at my vacuum and assured me I'd fallen prey to a snake oil salesman. While I waited, he replaced the belt, the roller, and several other indeterminate parts, making me wonder if I was in the process of falling prey to yet another snake oil salesman. It took one to know one, after all.

By the time I left the store my wallet was a lot lighter, but the repairman told me my vacuum was now in better condition than it had been when I bought it. Thinking back to the day I had let the salesman into the inn, due to my inability to say "no thanks," I thought of a very conceivable way to get a face-to-face meeting with the fireman, Sammy Saragusa, and I knew exactly where he lived. My conversation with Detective Travis earlier in the day convinced me it would be prudent to speak to the fireman.

I was aware of the fact I hadn't alerted either Wyatt or Stone of my intentions to go to a stranger's home by myself, but I felt it was something I needed to do. Surely, a fireman, even one who might be guilty of stealing toys, would not threaten me in any way. After all, a firefighter's goal was to save lives, not take them.

If I called Stone, he'd be upset and demand that I head straight home. I hadn't actually promised anything to either him or Wyatt, other than to not do anything even remotely dangerous. And, I certainly didn't consider this ruse I'd conjured up to be hazardous in any way, but just in case, I sent up a prayer for protection and drove south toward the turquoise house on Sycamore Street.

Sammy Saragusa worked the night shift at the fire station, so I knew there would be a good chance he'd be at home when I stopped by. His ex-wife had custody of their children, so it stood to reason he might have any stolen goods in his possession sitting out in the open. If nothing else, I could bring up the subject and see how Sammy responded to my questions. Maybe I could even get him to tell me where he'd been for those thirty minutes he'd been away from the station.

Luck was with me. I pulled in the drive and walked up to Sammy's front porch carrying my better-than-new vacuum. When an unimaginably handsome Italian man opened the door, I stood there in shocked silence, staring at the wet-haired Adonis who stood in front of me wearing nothing but a towel wrapped around his waist.

This man's abs were strung tighter than banjo strings. His tawny skin made me wonder if he frequented a tanning booth, and his well-toned body was radiating a musky, manly scent. I took a quick glance at my new wedding band to make sure my marriage of just six months was not just a long, vivid, and detailed dream. Which is not to say I'm irrational enough to think this hunky fireman would be interested in a woman old enough to be his mother, or that I was even on the same planet as him when it came to physical attractiveness.

"Um, I, um, well, um," I stopped babbling and swallowed hard before continuing. "I see I caught you at a bad time. I'll come back when it's more convenient for you."

"Oh, heck, come on in; now's as good a time as any." He opened the door wide for me, and although I tried to talk myself out of walking into his home, the young schoolgirl in me, salivating over the popular quarterback, came out, and I marched right into his living room, hoping he'd tucked the towel securely in place. I was sure the part of him covered by the towel was just as alluring as the rest of him, and even though I was still technically a newlywed, I was human and I could only take so much. Only death could prevent me from appreciating the masterpiece of the body God had gifted this man with.

"What can I do for you?" He asked. I shook my head to clear my mind before speaking.

"Well, I'm a door-to-door salesperson for the Talbot Vacuum Company and we are introducing the new Suckomatic H-200 to the citizens of Rockdale," I managed to get out.

"The Suckomatic?" He asked, with a dazzling bright

smile. "Well, I am in the market for a new vacuum cleaner, so why don't you tell me all about it."

I really only wanted to show him how it worked, look around for stolen toys, ask a few questions, and then beat it out of there before my eyes started burning from not blinking enough. I was finding it hard to take them off him for even the nanosecond it took to moisten them with a blink.

I certainly didn't want to sell him the vacuum cleaner that I now had over $700 invested in. I told myself then I'd have to try not to impress him much with the vacuum's performance. I didn't want to build it up as if it were the most amazing product to have ever hit the market, like the traveling salesman who sold it to me had done.

"Okay, Mr.," I stopped myself just in time before spitting his name out. As far as he was aware, I had no idea who he was or what he did for a living. "I'm sorry; I forgot to ask you what your name was."

We introduced ourselves, and I even gave him my real name in case we ever came in contact again in the future. Under most circumstances such as this, I would have made up a fictional name, but I didn't want to cause myself unnecessary embarrassment in the future. I was bound to run into him again, especially if I kept starting kitchen fires at the inn.

"Okay," I began. "Let me take a quick little peek around and see where the best place would be to demonstrate the capabilities of the Suckomatic H-200."

His adorable chuckle, when I mentioned the model name of the vacuum again, almost did me in. I could see this man on the front cover of the annual Firefighter's Calendar. For a split second, and against my better judgment, I willed the taut towel to come loose and drop to the floor. Then I shook my head, admonished myself for even letting that thought flit through my mind, and came back to my senses.

It was a small house, so it didn't take long to glance inside each room and do a quick scan of the contents. Apparently, his ex-wife, who must be one parasite short of a flea circus to have left this gorgeous man, had won all the furniture in the divorce settlement. I realize there's a lot more to making a relationship work than physical appearances, but with Sammy, it was a great start.

As I kept an eye out for any sign of toys that looked like they could have been pilfered from the storeroom at City Hall, I found nothing even remotely incriminating. I saw an older teddy bear in the corner of one bedroom, and that was the extent of anything child-related out in the open.

In fact, there was hardly any place to put the large box of toys where they could be hidden from sight. The closets were obviously of very limited size and capacity, not that I opened any doors to look inside, because that was pushing the privacy boundaries too far, even for an inquisitive individual like me.

I was fairly convinced Sammy Saragusa had not stolen the donated toys, but I had to carry out my ruse regardless. I chose a place in the corner of the living room, which contained one recliner, and an old-styled thirteen-inch television sitting on a wooden crate.

As I ran the vacuum cleaner over the carpet, I explained some of its features that I remembered from the snake oil salesman's spiel. I also punctuated my dialogue with comments such as, "I don't know why this thing is not picking up much today. It's usually at least a little more reliable than this. Or, at least it is when the belt is not smoking and stinking up the house."

"Belts can be easily replaced," Sammy said. "Besides, how often could that happen?"

"With the Suckomatic, it could happen more times than you can imagine. That's why I own a Bissell."

"Show me how it works," he said. "I'm not too particular when it comes to things like this. Motorcycles, yes. Women, even more so. But vacuum cleaners? Not so much."

"Okay. Well, I sure hope you aren't expecting too much in the way of performance. This thing's ridiculously expensive, but when it comes to suction and durability, it's mediocre at best." It was the worst sales pitch I could muster up, with no time to prepare an even more disparaging one, but my dismal description of the product I was supposedly trying to sell didn't seem to faze the fireman. He was a traveling salesman's dream; even more so than I am, and that was saying a lot.

After I gave a quick lackluster demonstration of the vacuum, which under the best of circumstances wasn't very impressive, Sammy said, "Yeah, I think this will work well enough for my needs."

"What?" I almost choked on my own saliva. "This thing's not cheap, you know. You could probably buy one that works twice as good, for less than half the cost at Wal-Mart or Target."

"How much is it?" He asked.

I hadn't thought that far ahead, never thinking for a minute he'd actually want to buy the silly thing. I wanted to make the price high enough to discourage Mr. Saragusa from wanting to purchase it, but I didn't have the heart to tell him it was a $600 machine, and would probably cost him a lot more in repair bills. I guess I was also a little embarrassed at how much I'd given for it, and couldn't own up to it even when I was trying *not* to sell it to someone else.

"Well, it is um, oh it's about, um, well, let's just say it's four hundred," I said, having developed a temporary speech impediment. "But I saw a very nice Hoover at Wal-Mart on sale for one-fifty. I'm sure it's all you really need for a house this size."

"Nah, I hate to shop. I'll just take the Suckomatic. It'll save me a trip to the store, and you're just too good a salesperson to resist," he said, with a sultry wink. I have to admit my heart skipped a beat, but I quickly realized it was the kind of bewitching gesture he probably handed out like candy to every middle-aged broad who looked like she hadn't been complimented by a sexy young man since the turn of the century.

Sammy Saragusa was definitely a charmer, but also a little bit stupid when it came to his finances. No wonder he was so far behind on his child-support payments. I figured that anyone who'd pay $400 for the heap of junk called a Suckomatic H-200, had very little sense. Then it occurred to me that I must not have a lick of sense myself, because I now had over $700 in the damn thing that wouldn't suck up a paper clip if its life depended on it. And worse yet, I was now selling the expensive piece of junk for a lot less than I'd just recently invested in it!

"Will you take a check?" He asked. "I used up most of my cash to buy a couple toys for this collection deal they've got going at work. But I'm pretty sure the check's good. Or, at least, if you hold it for a few days it should clear the bank."

"Yeah, whatever," I said. "Just leave the 'payable to' line blank and I'll use the company stamp on it."

The situation was bad enough as it was, and I didn't want to have to try to cash a check made out to the Talbot Vacuum Company. If nothing else came out of this encounter, at least I was fairly convinced a guy who would spend what little cash he had on toys to donate to needy children, was not guilty of the crime of stealthily stealing other people's contributions from the storeroom.

Sammy wrote me a check that I was praying wasn't from an account with insufficient funds. If the check bounced, I wasn't sure I'd have the nerve to go back to his house and demand cash. Oh well, I'd already wasted $300 on a useless painting, so what was another $700 if I ended up giving the vacuum away for nothing? I didn't even want to think about how many toys I could buy with a thousand bucks. It would way more than replace all the ones that had been stolen.

But, I was quick to remind myself that it wasn't the value of the stolen toys that bothered me. It was the principle of the thing, and the fact some freak of nature would do something so cruel to little children and get away scot-free, with no repercussions at all.

I didn't want to explain to Stone how or why I had returned to the inn without the vacuum, so I made a side trip to Wal-Mart to purchase the Hoover I'd seen on sale. It was the same one I had tried to convince Sammy he should buy for himself. I would tell Stone I'd made an exchange at the vacuum store. He wouldn't give it a second thought. Vacuum cleaners and their value weren't something he spent a lot of time thinking about.

I really needed to either discover who the thief was soon, or give up trying before I drained my own checking account. My investigative efforts so far had been very expensive!

CHAPTER 5

There was no mention of the vacuum cleaner when I returned to the inn. I don't think Stone even realized that I'd come home with a different vacuum than I'd left the inn with earlier. But then, I suppose if he had left with a Zebco Rod and Reel, and returned with a Berkley combo, I wouldn't have noticed the difference either. In fact, after he'd left my sight for fifteen seconds, I usually couldn't even recall what color shirt he was wearing. It was either a matter of perspective...or the onset of Alzheimer's.

I noticed the message light blinking on the house phone when I walked into the kitchen. It was Wyatt asking if either Stone or I had time to run over to the city hall building to empty the collection bin located up near the front desk. It was close to overflowing, he said.

I had several days off from working at the library. I'd been training a new lady, with a lot of past librarian experience, to take over the reins as head librarian. My temporary librarian stint had run its course. The new hire had required very little orientation, and had quickly picked up on the little intricacies that were specific to the Rockdale Public Library. I'd decided to give her a few days to run the library without my assistance, with the assurance I was but a phone call away if she were to run into something she needed help with.

So far the new librarian had not run across any situation she couldn't handle herself, and with her level of competency, I didn't anticipate that she would. It had been a case of perfect timing, because it freed me up to look into the toy theft and to catch up on some chores around the inn.

Stone had left to go look at a new electric fertilizer-spreader attachment for his mower, but I had plenty of spare time to run over and collect the toys. I grabbed a turkey sandwich and a cup of coffee for lunch, and then drove over to City Hall. Hopefully I'd be able to stuff all the donations into my back and passenger seats. If not, I thought, I could always make two trips.

As it turned out, my Volkswagen Beetle would only hold a little more than half of what had been collected in just the last few days. I was overwhelmed by the kindness and generosity of the townspeople in their willingness to help others who were less fortunate than they were. Why would Sammy Saragusa, or anyone else for that matter, ever want to move away from such a benevolent community?

When I returned to City Hall to collect the remainder of the items in the collection bin, I walked down the right wing to the police station, hoping to catch Wyatt and let him know I'd taken care of the task of emptying the bin. Right before the door to the large room, where Wyatt had told me each officer had a desk for taking care of their paperwork, was an office with a placard on the door that read *Leonard Smith, Chief of Police*.

I knew this might be my only chance to speak to him about the theft of the Christmas toys from the storeroom.

What would it hurt to step into his office and ask him a few questions? I'd known Chief Smith from my involvement with the previous cases I'd taken it upon myself to investigate. I'd found myself on his shit list on more than one occasion, but we still had a mutual respect for each other.

Perhaps I should rephrase my last statement. I had a great deal of respect for the Chief of Police, and due to my success in tracking down killers in the past, he *should* have a great deal of respect for me, as well. Truth be told, he likely thought I was just a nosy ninny who occasionally got lucky in my attempts to solve a case I had no business investigating. Not only did he probably not have one ounce of respect for me, but also could barely tolerate me. But he did present me with a Certificate of Appreciation just a few weeks ago, so that was worth a lot in my totally unbiased opinion.

I knocked softly on the chief's door, waited a few moments, and then knocked louder when he didn't respond to the lighter rapping. When he failed to answer my second knock, I opened the door slowly and looked around to see if Chief Smith was at his desk.

The room was empty, and after spending less than ten seconds debating the wisdom and legality of entering his room unannounced, and uninvited, I walked on in and shut the door behind me.

I don't know what I hoped to discover by scrutinizing the items on top of his desk, but I found nothing of any significance. I told myself I wouldn't read anything that looked personal or important to the welfare of the city. Leonard Smith was a neat freak, and I always admired that trait in others, because it was one I completely lacked. There were several perfectly aligned stacks of documents and paperwork distributed in a fashion that indicated it was not a random placement.

The only thing that looked out of place was a post-it note stuck to the handset of his desk phone. It read

Rachel 3:00. I glanced at my watch and noted that it was about two-forty-five, and assumed Chief Smith had left to meet this woman somewhere in about fifteen minutes. So I also assumed I would have free rein of the chief's office for at least a short while. *Assuming* things had gotten me in trouble more times than I could count, but it never stopped me from doing it again and again on a regular basis.

I noticed a door leading to what was obviously a large closet. If this lawman had stolen the gifts, which I found extremely difficult to fathom, might he have hidden them away in his office closet until Christmas? I knew his own children were grown, but there was a reasonable possibility of him and his wife having grandkids.

I didn't truly cast any aspersions on Chief Smith, not ever seriously considering him a suspect in this case. But since I was there, and had the opportunity, why not spend just a few seconds looking in the closet before getting the hell out of there? I wanted to vacate the chief of police's office before I got caught red-handed. It was a short walk to where I would be arrested, booked, and fingerprinted. Trespassing on police property, and actively investigating and snooping on the man in charge of the entire Rockdale police force, were factors that would not bode well with a jury of my peers.

I suddenly had a sense of foreboding, and almost immediately felt my knees nearly buckle when I heard someone opening the office door and stepping inside the room. I quickly pulled the closet door shut. Could the chief have forgotten or canceled his three o'clock meeting? Or was it someone else entirely who was just passing through, maybe to lay a police report on his desk? I prayed silently for the latter.

Sometimes our prayers go unanswered for whatever reason. I heard the chair being pulled away from the desk, and the squeaky sound of old wood, as the pressure of someone weighing in the neighborhood of two-fifty, sat down on it.

Crap! I thought. Who would have the courage or gall to sit down at the boss's desk, other than the big kahuna himself? What if he needed to get something out of his closet? I didn't even want to consider the ramifications of that possibility.

Before I could conjure up an escape plan, I heard the distinct sound of a rotary phone being dialed. Rotary phone? Really? And I thought I had come into this century kicking and screaming. Had the police department really not advanced to something a touch more modern in the past twenty or thirty years?

I then heard Leonard Smith's voice as he spoke into the phone. I had to place my ear tightly to the door to make out his words.

"Rachel?" He asked. "Are you alone?"

I couldn't hear the other end of the conversation, but the gist of it was that the chief was making arrangements to meet Rachel after work for a drink before proceeding to the Waldorf Hotel in Saint Joseph later on that evening. The no-good scoundrel told Rachel he'd tell his wife he had a long and involved meeting with the mayor after work that he expected would last for several hours.

Wow! I thought. Who would have ever thought that this man, held in great regard by the majority of Rockdale's citizens, would have another, darker side to him? Furthermore, what would he do to someone he found hiding in his closet, and eavesdropping on this scandalous conversation? It was certain to change his life irreparably if news of his clandestine affair got out.

The last thing I wanted to do was alert either Wyatt or Stone of my location and situation, but I was in no position to stay in the chief's closet and wait for a miracle to happen. Our Lord was acclaimed for turning water into wine and feeding the masses with five loaves of bread and two fishes. But I'd not read one testament in the Bible of him rescuing a foolish lunatic from a closet she had no business being in to begin with.

After trying to think of any possible way to get out of my current messy situation without bringing two overly protective men into the picture, I finally had to give in and call for help. If I called Wyatt, I reasoned, and spoke as quietly as possible, maybe he could think of a way to get the chief out of his office long enough for me to escape undetected. Naturally, there'd be hell to pay when I got home, but it wouldn't be the first time, and I'd just have to cry, plead, and beg for forgiveness when the time came. It was a routine I knew only too well.

I could tell the chief was now talking to his wife, explaining the meeting he had with the mayor that evening that only he, Rachel, and myself, knew he had no attention of attending. I felt this might be my best chance to call Wyatt, while Chief Smith was engrossed with telling a bald-faced lie to his spouse.

Whispering into my cell phone to Wyatt, I explained briefly my current location and my need for his help. The detective was obviously not pleased with me, but I hadn't expected that he would be.

"Good grief, Lexie! Haven't you learned anything in the past couple of years? Did you inform Stone of your plans?"

I murmured negatively, and after listening to a few more unflattering remarks and attacks on my character, Wyatt told me to hang tight, and he'd think of something. Knowing he'd batted a thousand getting me out of trouble before, I felt greatly relieved.

That sense of relief heightened significantly when I heard Detective Clint Travis enter the room and ask the chief if he'd accompany him out to the parking lot to look at an unexplained dent in his patrol car. Apparently, Wyatt had gotten Detective Travis to assist him in rescuing me, or so I thought. Once again I felt a pang of guilt that my first impression of Clint Travis, a month or so ago, had not been favorable to the detective.

The sense of relief fizzled and panic set in when I heard Chief Smith say, "Let me get my camera out of the closet. We'll have to have photos for the accident report."

The closet was large, but so well organized there was no place to hide. My actions had been unnecessary, because there wasn't a toy or anything remotely suspicious on any of the shelves. That only served to make it more maddening that I was about to be caught in a very awkward position, and no doubt, escorted to the county jail by a man who'd probably be more than happy to see me arrested and put away for life.

Just as I stepped back to await my fate, a very loud fire alarm went off in the building. It was so deafening I wondered if the loudspeaker was in the chief's office. But I didn't wonder long, because in the process of stepping back, and being scared spitless by the unexpected blaring, I tripped and fell backward, striking my head on a metal shelf at the rear of the closet.

The next thing I recalled was waking up in a partitioned-off cubicle in the emergency room, a place I recognized immediately from my many visits there. A nurse on duty was inserting an IV into my forearm. Wyatt was running his hand across the back of my head. I heard him speaking to the doctor that was standing beside me.

"That's quite a goose egg she has on the back of her head. She's lucky she didn't split her skull open. Do you think she'll be all right?" Wyatt asked.

The physician was nodding when I opened my eyes and tried to focus on him. "Yeah, but she'll probably have a hell of a headache. I'm pretty sure she has a concussion, but there shouldn't be any long term damage."

"That's a relief," Wyatt said. When he noticed my eyes were open, he asked me how I felt.

"What happened?" I asked, with a voice that sounded like someone else's inside my head. It was so unnerving I wasn't even sure I was the one who had spoken.

"We'll talk about it later," he replied. Obviously, he didn't want our conversation to be heard by the emergency room physician. I'm sure what he had to relate to me was incriminating to Wyatt, myself, or both of us. "I'll tell you all about it when I get you back to the inn. I tried to contact Stone, but he didn't answer his phone."

As the doctor had predicted, I had a pounding headache. I didn't want to even think about what Wyatt was going to tell me, or how Stone would react to the news. I didn't want to think about it. I didn't want to fret over it. And I didn't want to let Wyatt know how anxious I was about Stone's reaction. I only wanted to close my eyes and visualize myself soaking up the sun, while lying on a chaise lounge at water's edge, as I was vacationing on some exotic Caribbean island. Anything to take my mind off my predicament and what the evening would bring in the way of marital discourse.

I was wishing the pain killer medicine the nurse had given me intravenously would kick in soon. In the meantime, I was forced to once again visualize myself soaking up the sun, while laying on a chaise lounge at water's edge, but with the worse blinding headache that I'd ever had in my fifty years of life.

It was not an easy decision for me to make, but I knew it was the right one. I was going to give up my quest to find out who stole the toys from the storeroom. I had to let it go and devote my time and energy to turning the librarian position over to the new hire, and getting everything prepared for the Christmas celebration at the Alexandria Inn.

CHAPTER 6

Stone surprised me, as he often did, with his reaction when Wyatt brought me back to the inn from the Heartland Memorial Hospital in St. Joseph. After Detective Johnston explained to Stone what had happened, Stone's entire focus was on my condition. He was more concerned with the aftereffects of the concussion I'd incurred than with what had precipitated my injury.

That's not to say a lot of groaning, frowning, and eye rolling didn't go on while Wyatt related the story to him. Although I was being granted a respite, I wasn't apt to be let off the hook entirely. I made certain to tell him I was through investigating the theft of the donated toys, hoping to temper the lecture that was sure to come eventually, once I was in better condition to pay attention to his words of dismay and disappointment.

I was bound to hear how much Stone loved me, and how devastated he'd be if something happened to me. Under normal circumstances, I thoroughly enjoyed and appreciated his kind, loving words, but not so much when it was meant to make me feel ashamed of my reckless and impulsive behavior.

However, I couldn't complain about Stone being over-protective of me. The fact that he put up with my shenanigans in situations like this was probably way more than I deserved. Coupled with the fact that, despite my shenanigans, he continued to love me, and want to protect me from harm, made me a very lucky lady. Nonetheless, you could bet I was going to milk this injury for as long as I could to put off the inevitable.

Wyatt explained to us that just as he approached the chief's office earlier, Clint Travis was opening the door to go into the room to speak with Chief Smith.

"I knew I had to come up with plan B immediately. There was no way I could go into the chief's office and interrupt their discussion," Wyatt said.

"You didn't send Detective Travis into the chief's office in order to lure Chief Smith away from his office?" I asked. I had assumed Clint was in on the scheme, particularly after he asked the chief to go outside and look at a dent in his patrol car.

"No, he really did discover a dent in his back fender, which he needed to bring to Chief Smith's attention. I didn't want to make an accessory out of any of my co-workers, even Clint, and the more people involved, the more apt my actions were to come back and bite me in the ass," he replied.

I knew Wyatt was right, and I felt bad I'd had to put him in the position of putting his neck, and job, on the line for me. I couldn't adequately express how grateful I was to the detective, and how relieved I was that he didn't end up in a serious jam because of me.

"You are such a great friend, Wyatt. I promise to always have coffee and pastries waiting for you whenever you drop by the inn from here on out. I'm curious about something, though. You must have set off the fire alarm yourself, didn't you?" I asked.

"Yes, I did," Wyatt replied. "We have a strict protocol we're supposed to follow when the fire alarm goes off. The fire department is stationed in the same building, but everybody has to evacuate and wait outside until the danger has passed. When Chief Smith and Detective Travis left the office to go outside, as everyone is required to do, I rushed in behind them and found you unconscious in the closet. At the time, I wasn't sure what had happened to you, so I called for an EMT to meet us in the fire station, and I carried you down there. He's the one who advised me to take you straight to the emergency ward to be checked out. One of the ER nurses told me the staff there was beginning to wonder if you'd moved away from the area because they hadn't treated you for over a month."

"Yeah, yeah, the emergency room staff gets way too much amusement out of teasing me. Chuck, one of the male nurses, asked me today if I claimed the hospital as my second home on my income tax returns. They should all be stand-up comedians when they're not saving lives," I said.

"But thank God for those comedians!" Stone said. "We've needed their help a number of times in the last year or two. In fact, I think Lexie has been their best customer."

"Oh, jeez, they're wearing off on you now. Say, Wyatt, did you catch any flack for setting off the alarm, or does anyone even know it was you who did it?" I asked out of curiosity, and also fear that I'd caused undue problems for the detective who'd become such a close friend of ours.

"No, I radioed the chief and told him it was a false alarm. I told him I thought I smelled smoke and decided it was better to be safe than sorry. He didn't even flinch at my explanation. I was afraid I may have been caught on video tripping the alarm on one of the security cameras, and if I didn't own up to it, they'd think I did it as a prank. If that happened, I knew I'd probably be working at the convenience store as a clerk next week. As it turned out, I found out the security cameras were still malfunctioning."

"Well, I can't tell you how much I appreciate you saving my bacon once again," I said sincerely.

Stone and Wyatt began discussing the upcoming football game between the Kansas City Chiefs and the St. Louis Rams, and which team they thought was going to win the Missouri Governor's Cup, as the contest was called whenever these two teams met.

The back of my head was sore and I desperately wanted to go lie down and take a nap. I told the men I was going upstairs to rest.

Stone shook his head at me, and said, "I don't think you're suppose to sleep for awhile after suffering a concussion."

"I talked to Jim, the EMT who's a friend of mine, about that very subject, and he told me it is now considered perfectly safe as long as the patient isn't displaying symptoms such as trouble walking or dilated pupils," Wyatt explained to both Stone and me. I noticed he looked straight at my eyes as he spoke. "But, just for the heck of it, Stone, you might go up in an hour or so and check on her."

I felt totally dejected as I slowly climbed the stairs up to our suite. So far, I'd bought an ugly, but expensive painting, had most likely given my even more expensive vacuum cleaner away for nothing, and put my friend's job in jeopardy, not to mention nearly busting my skull in two, all in a futile attempt to bring a toy thief to justice. I thought briefly about going back to the ER, because I really did need to have my head examined—again! But this time to see if they could detect anything in there but cobwebs and dust bunnies!

CHAPTER 7

I spent the next day taking pain pills every four hours to ward off the excruciating headache that still lingered, while preparing the inn for our Christmas celebration. Stone went to a tree lot and brought home a beautifully shaped Blue Spruce that stood almost ten feet tall, to set up in our parlor, which sported a twelve-foot ceiling.

I was decorating the tree when Wendy stopped by to see how I was recuperating from my head injury. She must have either been in the sauce, or just delirious with holiday spirit, because she didn't start right off with disrespectful comments about my experience in the city hall building the previous day.

"Stone found a gorgeous tree this year," she commented. "Do you need help with the decorations?"

I thanked her and told her I had it under control, and then asked her if she and Veronica had decided on a menu for our Christmas supper. As I'd anticipated, they were planning on roasting a large turkey and serving it with all the trimmings. It was going to be quite a feast, she told me.

"What would you like me to prepare for the meal?" I asked. I wasn't surprised when Wendy assured me that she and Veronica could handle the entire meal themselves. I wasn't sure if she was keeping me out of the meal preparations because of my concussion, or because she was afraid that I would screw up anything assigned to me, including opening up the cranberry sauce jar. But I didn't care either way. I had a lot of other things to take care of, like wrapping all the Christmas gifts, including dozens of toys for the kids, and renting a Santa Claus costume for Stone.

After discussing the need for a costume with my daughter, she called *The Party Palace*, a new shop down on Main Street, three doors down from the vacuum cleaner dealer. Wendy reserved a suit over the phone because it was the only one available at such a late date, and she didn't want to take the chance it would be rented out before we could get to the store.

"Give me your credit card, Mom, and I'll go pick it up," she volunteered.

"Oh, that would be wonderful, honey. Thanks for your help. I'm still a little dazed from taking such a hard blow to my head."

"No problem," Wendy said. "I should also get a few brownie points for not raking you over the coals about the little *mishap* that took place yesterday."

I had figured I wouldn't get off scot-free, so I just smiled and changed the subject. "While you're out, can you pick up the last bunch of donations from Pete's Pantry, and ask them to put the collection bin back in their stock room?"

"Sure," she agreed. I thanked her and sent her on her way before she remembered she'd been about to get up on her soapbox to lecture me about my mind-numbing recklessness, and the fact I didn't have the sense God gave the pine cone I was hanging from a branch on the

Christmas tree.

Later that afternoon, Wendy and I were sorting through the last batch of donations. I was separating the toys from the food and household items. I'd already selected all the toys for Seth, Hailey, and Dax, as well as Coral's kids. Coral had told me her daughter, Anna Mae was eight, and her son, Justin, was five. I had picked out appropriate toys for each child, but I still had to go to Best Buy in St. Joseph to pick up two Xbox 360's, and a couple of Kindle Fires for Abbie and Coral. I also wanted to purchase a fifty-dollar Amazon gift card for each of the ladies to go toward eBooks for their electronic reading devices.

As I was thinking about things I needed to accomplish in the next few days, Wendy brought me out of my reverie when she exclaimed, "Holy crap!"

"What's up?" I asked her.

"I just found this red Furby amongst all the donated toys! Remember me telling you they were the hot toy of the season and almost impossible to find? I can't believe someone was able to find one, and then donated it to the cause."

"If it's that special, we need to give it to Hailey Allen. She's seven, and probably the perfect age to enjoy it," I said. Wendy agreed and set it aside before continuing to sort through the donations.

The next day was a busy one for me. Stone used his truck to take another load of toys to Leavenworth to donate to the Toys for Tots program. He'd been taking a batch to them about every fourth day during our collection drive. After that, we'd only have one final batch to transport to Leavenworth.

I made two trips in my VW Bug to the food bank with the last bunch of food and household items. They were delighted to see me, as the shelves were being stripped almost as fast as they were being restocked.

The volunteer, a young man in his thirties, said, "Business is always brisk right before the holidays. With the economy in the toilet, a lot of people are struggling this holiday season. This is my fourth year as a volunteer here at the food bank, and I've never seen our supplies so low."

I was always happy to see young people giving back to their communities, and helping others in any way they could. My holiday spirit was ramping up with Christmas just days away, so I took out my checkbook and wrote a check for $300 to help support the food bank, which played such a vital role in Rockdale. The way I was going through money the last few days, it was fortunate for me that my late first husband, Chester, had left me financially sound.

And, I decided that if I could throw away that much money on a painting that looked like someone had thrown up on a canvas, I could surely donate that much to such a worthy cause. It was not only tax deductible, it was also the right thing to do. And as I was discovering, giving to others was what the Christmas spirit was all about.

After I left the food bank, I drove to St. Joseph to purchase the video game devices, Kindles, and gift cards at Best Buy, and on my way home I was thinking about the coveted Furby someone had been generous enough to donate to a local family in need.

Like a lightning bolt from the sky, I was struck by an idea I felt had at least a reasonable chance of solving the toy theft case. I pulled off the road into the parking lot of a convenience store. First, I went inside to use the restroom to get rid of my last cup of coffee, and purchase a fresh cup to replace it.

Then I utilized the Internet browser on my smart phone to search for a tracking device that might work for my idea. I found an Amber Alert GPS device that you could put in your child's backpack or clothing, and using a phone like mine, you could always detect exactly where they were at any given time. If it could track the whereabouts of a child, why couldn't it also do the same with a Furby?

I thought that if I put the device inside the interactive doll, either in the battery compartment if possible or I sewed it into the interior, I could follow the movement of the Furby if I could entice the scumbag to steal it. Being the hottest, hard-to-find toy of the season, it would be a big draw for a toy thief. I quickly called Wyatt and ran my idea by him. The collection bin was nearly full in the city hall building, and Wyatt had planned to empty it that afternoon. He was going to bring the contents to the Alexandria Inn, while moving the empty container to the storeroom because the collection period was drawing to a close.

If we could leave the full container in place for a couple more days, and I could rig the Furby with one of the tracking devices, we could place it in full view on the top of the bin full of toys. Then Wyatt could spread it around the city hall, as much as possible, that one of the most wanted toys of the year had just been placed in the collection bin. Maybe we could tempt the thief to steal one more very popular toy. This toy could lead us right to the thief's doorstep.

Wyatt was skeptical, but agreed to do as I requested. He suggested we keep the fact the toy was rigged with a tracking device entirely to ourselves, so that only Wyatt, Stone, and I knew about its existence. The fewer people who knew about it the better. There would be less chance of the set-up leaking out.

The thief would be an instant hero to his kid, or kids, if he were able to give them this most desirous item that was on almost every child's wish list. The elusive Furby might just prove to be too much of a temptation for the toy snatcher to resist.

After I got Wyatt to agree to assist me in my crafty little ploy, I ordered the tracking device, and paid a ridiculous amount for express delivery. It was guaranteed to arrive before noon the next day.

I was so thrilled with my plan that I almost ran two or three vehicles off the road and missed a pedestrian by mere inches. The man looked up at me and used his right hand to show me his opinion of me. Oh well, I thought, it's not like I hadn't been the target of that gesture several times before. I had bigger fish to fry, and no time to dwell on a rude pedestrian, even if I did nearly run him over in broad daylight.

Like a child eager for Santa Claus to arrive, I was anxiously awaiting the UPS man the following morning. I had the red Furby in pre-op, ready to be sliced open for its tracking device implant. The Furby, who I'd dubbed Frank, was resting comfortably, unaware of his ensuing surgery and the mission he was about to undertake.

After I'd gone to the kitchen window above the sink for about the fortieth time to watch for a big brown truck to come rolling down the driveway, Stone suggested I join him on the back porch for a cup of coffee. Naturally, this was an offer I was physically unable to refuse. Stone knows my weakness, and he's not afraid to use it against me.

Sitting on the back porch with Stone, feeding my caffeine addiction, we discussed the toy heist, and Frank Furby's chances of bringing down the perpetrator. Stone seemed almost as excited about the cunning plot as I was.

"What do you plan to do with Frank if your idea works?" Stone asked.

"I had originally planned to give it to Bailey Allen as a gift from Santa. But I'm afraid this surgery Frank's about to undergo might render him unable to talk, dance, or do anything other than lie there like a furry owl-looking doll in a coma. I'm afraid a child might find a vegetative Furby a bit disappointing."

"Yeah, I guess you're right," Stone said with a chuckle. "How about if we find a prominent place to display him in the parlor every holiday season as a reminder of Christmas's past? After all, he's red; a color very much associated with this time of year, and if your plan is successful, Frank will lend a very significant meaning to this special Christmas season."

The more I thought about Stone's suggestion, the more I liked it. It would bring back memories, for sure, even some I wasn't sure I wanted to be reminded of year after year. As we chatted about mundane things like his tighty-whities that I'd turned pink in the laundry, my inability to whistle, and the huge spider web under the patio table that I'd been too lazy to do anything about, one cup of coffee turned in to two, and then three.

Before I knew it, an hour had passed without me once thinking about the UPS man's arrival. So I was taken by surprise when there was a loud rapping on the front door.

"I think your boyfriend's here," Stone said. He always teased me about how often UPS, Fed-X, and the postal service, delivered packages to the inn. He said he was beginning to think I had the hots for men in uniforms. Actually, it was just a matter of me being almost as addicted to eBay and Amazon as I was to coffee. I rarely left the inn to buy anything any more. Why waste the time and gas when my next purchase was but a click away? As it turned out the UPS "man" was a lady, but I would have kissed her anyway if I weren't afraid she'd think an unstable dingbat was molesting her.

The surgery went well. Outwardly, Frank looked none the worse for wear, other than a slight bulge on his left side that would surely go unnoticed by anyone unfamiliar with the toy, who would surely be in a rush to grab it and go. Even though the Furby's internal injuries were severe, he was still up for the job of nabbing a toy thief. Wyatt had been called and was on his way to the inn to pick up Frank and take him to the city hall building and place him on top of the collection bin, which was nearly overflowing already.

I had cherry tarts, Wyatt's favorite, set out on a plate for him. I was deeply in debt to the detective and had made him a promise I intended to keep. I would keep the sweets coming from this day forward. Not that I hadn't been doing that all along, as was evident by my ever-expanding waistline.

After the detective visited with us briefly, and commented on how hideously ugly Frank was, he took the toy and headed back to City Hall. But before he left, the three of us discussed the furtive plan we had set into motion.

"I will get the rumor mill up and running as soon as I get there. By the end of the workday everyone in the building will know that one of the most coveted toys of the year, which was nearly impossible to find anywhere in the area, had been donated to our charity drive," Wyatt said.

"I just hope it was an employee at the city services building who stole the toys, or the plan won't work," I said.

"I'd say the chances are good, because otherwise, they probably wouldn't have known about the storeroom, or even that the toys were being stored there. I'll also spread around the fact that the bin was due to be emptied soon because the collection drive was coming to an end. I'll just say I want everyone to know if they had anything they wanted to donate, the time was running out to do so."

"Good idea, Wyatt," I said. "We want to add a sense of urgency to the matter, because we don't know how long the batteries will last in the GPS device I've implanted in Frank's belly."

"I might even have Lola announce over the loudspeaker that there were only a couple of days left of the collection drive if anyone still wants to contribute. It's not uncommon for her to make announcements about things of that nature, so it won't seem out of the ordinary to anyone or throw up any red flags," Wyatt continued. I could tell the detective was anxious to see if the scheme worked too. The three of us were almost giddy with excitement as we discussed the subterfuge we were executing.

As the detective picked up the red doll to head back to the station, I hugged Wyatt and kissed Frank, and wished them both luck. I am embarrassed to admit I found myself a little sad to see Frank leave, knowing if the plan failed, he might have been maimed for no reason, and we may never see him again. I'd never been this emotionally attached to a doll when I was a young girl, so I blamed my sentimentality about Frank on my recent head injury.

As you can imagine, I spent the rest of the day pacing, glancing at the clock, and looking at my smart phone. I wrapped the last few gifts and placed them under the tree. It had become obvious I'd overdone it, and the children were going to be overwhelmed with toys on Christmas Day. But, I thought it might help ease the pain of missing their father this holiday season.

And from speaking to Coral, I discovered Anna Mae and Justin's father was out of the picture. He not only made no effort to see and spend time with his own children, but he also made no effort to make his child support payments to the mother of his children. Coral's children could probably use a little boost to their spirits too, and I hoped our Christmas celebration would accomplish that goal.

I was reflecting back to how warm and loving my

parents were, and how they had made our holidays so special. My parents, now both deceased, were not well off, but we didn't care about the quality or quantity of our presents. We just enjoyed celebrating the season as a family. Mom and Dad always made sure we remembered what Christmas was really all about. Mom would read us a story about the birth of Christ, and we would light candles in his honor. I had carried on the tradition with my own daughter, and knew Wendy would continue to do so with her own children some day.

As I daydreamed about the past, I almost didn't notice the Amber Alert monitor indicating that the Furby was on the move. I knew none of us had moved the doll, so assumed it had probably been pilfered from the collection bin, and was now apparently traveling down Mimosa Avenue.

Hang in there, Frank; I'm coming to rescue you! I thought with glee. I quickly called Wyatt, and he told me I should be outside and ready to go when he arrived at the inn to pick me up. Much to Wyatt's dismay, I had insisted on being involved in the chase, and the eventual apprehension of the toy-napper. I don't know why he was so surprised at my determination to ride along in the police car. Did he not know me better than that by now?

As I watched the monitor on my smart phone, an app that had been downloaded to communicate with the device inside Frank, I gave instructions to Wyatt. I sat in the back seat, while Detective Clint Travis's partner, Detective Russell, sat in the front passenger seat. Detective Travis had just left the building to go out on patrol, but Russell had offered to ride along with Wyatt.

I was glad to see Wyatt had brought backup; not that I expected a shoot-out would occur, but it was always better to be over-manned than under-manned in a situation like this. Who knew if the perpetrator would be armed, or stupid enough to try to shoot his way out of what was not the sort of crime likely to result in a lot of jail time in the first place.

"Turn right on Spruce Street," I said from the back seat. "Go two blocks west and turn right again on Maple."

The monitor indicated the Furby had stopped moving. When I told Wyatt, he said, "The thief is probably at his home now. I can't believe it, but I think your sly little scheme is going to work, Lexie!"

My heart began to beat in double time as we got closer and closer to the device, which was still sending out a signal. When we pulled up in front of a small, drab-looking white house, with a "For Sale by Owner" sign in front of it, Wyatt exclaimed, "Oh my God! I would never have imagined this!"

"What?" Detective Russell and I asked in unison.

"You're not going to believe who lives here. This house is owned by the security guard, Willie Cooper!"

"Are you serious?" I asked in total disbelief.

"Unfortunately, yes, I'm very serious," Wyatt said, with a touch of sadness in his voice. "He's the last person on earth I would ever have expected to do something like this. Stealing toys from kids is just not in his nature, or so I thought, anyway."

Wyatt pulled the patrol car into Willie Cooper's driveway, and when he and Michael Russell stepped out of the patrol car, I saw the window blinds open up and someone peer out through the slats. Shortly afterward, Mr. Cooper stepped out on his front porch with his hands up in the air, and the most remorseful expression I've ever seen on a person's face. His head hung down in shame. He put his hands behind his back and turned around on his own accord to allow Wyatt to cuff him without incident.

Wyatt hesitated, and looked up at Detective Russell with a questioning look. Russell shrugged, and then slowly nodded. It was clear that Wyatt didn't feel right cuffing the man, but he reluctantly did so, and led the retired policeman, and now City Hall security guard, to the patrol car. Wyatt helped Willie into the back seat, and motioned for me to sit up front while Russell sat in the back with the suspect.

As we headed back toward the police station, Willie began apologizing to everyone in the car. There were tears running down his cheeks as he explained what had prompted him to steal the toys from the storeroom. Tears began to well up in my own eyes as he spoke. I even saw Wyatt reach up to wipe a tear off his cheek.

"I didn't mean to hurt anyone," Willie began. "But as I watched the collection bin fill to its full capacity time after time, I could tell there were going to be way more than enough toys for one family, no matter how many children they had. I wanted to ask if there was any way that some of the excess toys could be donated to the orphanage I support. There are six children living there right now, waiting for families of their own, and I wanted to brighten their spirits with a nice Christmas, but things are so tight right now it didn't look possible. The downturn in the economy has hurt so many people that the donations to the orphanage have trickled down to such a degree that I had to begin selling everything I owned on eBay to generate money to keep it operating."

"Mr. Cooper," I said. "Why didn't you ask us for some of the toys? We'd have been more than happy to donate all you needed for the orphans."

"I guess I just didn't feel it was my place to do so, as the collection drive had been set up for another family in need. I was going to ask until I heard you intended to donate the excess toys to the Leavenworth Toys for Tots program, and I figured if you wanted the orphanage to have a few of them, you would have offered."

"Oh, my goodness," I replied. "I'm so sorry, Mr. Cooper, I feel awful for not even thinking of the orphanage's need for toys. We had plenty to go around.

We could have supplied the orphans with dozens of Christmas gifts, and still had a lot left to donate to Toys for Tots. I guess I was just too pre-occupied with other things to think of it."

"I know it was wrong of me to do what I did," Willie said with a sniff. "I just didn't want to let the kids down, and I thought a few toys would not be missed, considering the amount pouring in for the collection drive. I decided I'd rather take a chance on getting caught and ruining my own life, than to make theirs even worse than they'd already experienced in their short lives. I'm truly sorry. I admit I even sold some of the most expensive items on eBay to help keep the kids fed until I could think of another way to generate funds. I knew I could get a good amount for the Furby, so I couldn't resist taking one last toy. I'm so very, very sorry. I was desperate and I didn't know what else to do. I deserve whatever happens to me at this point. I just hope someone will step in and help out at the orphanage while I'm incarcerated. Those kids have nowhere else to go. The orphanage is the only home they know."

I looked up and saw that we were a block away from the police station. In a matter of minutes, they would be leading Willie Cooper into the police station to arrest and book him. His fate would be in the justice system's hands from that point forward. The orphans would be left to fend for themselves, and no doubt feel as if they'd been "re-orphaned" when their only parent figure was taken away from them.

"Stop the car, Wyatt!" I said. "Can we pull over to the curb for a minute?"

Wyatt looked more than happy to do as I requested. He had been driving slower and slower the closer we got to the police station, as if trying to put off the inevitable.

"Do we really have to take Mr. Cooper to the police station?" I asked. "I know I personally have no intentions of pressing charges against him. I realize, as does he, that what he did was wrong, but I also know he did it for all the right reasons. I should have offered to help, and I still intend to, but I can't bear to think of those poor children with no families to call their own, having to deal with the loss of their leader, a man who cares more about their welfare than his own. And it totally breaks my heart to see them even more devastated during the holiday season by allowing this to happen. These children not having gifts under the tree, will pale in comparison to what might happen if Mr. Cooper is arrested and booked into the county jail."

"I agree whole-heartedly with you, Lexie," Wyatt said, his relief very evident. Then the detective turned around in his seat to face Mr. Cooper, and said. "Willie, if you promise not to ever steal anything again and we offer to help you out in any way we can, I will drive you back to your house, and this will go no further than here. As they say in Las Vegas, what happens in this police car stays in this police car. Do you promise? I don't want to see you stealing anything again, because those kids need you and I don't want to see you rotting away in a jail cell when you should be helping those orphans find permanent homes."

"Oh, I promise, I most earnestly promise, and I mean that with every fiber of my being," Willie said. As with Wyatt, Mr. Cooper's own extreme relief was etched in every line and wrinkle on his face. I will give you back all the toys as soon as we get to my house. The kids will just have to do without this year."

"The kids will do no such thing!" I exclaimed. "Those toys are going to them, including any more that you need. We still have a final batch of toys to do something with, and I'm sure the Toys for Tots organization would be more than happy to see them go to your orphanage. They are in the business of making every needy child's Christmas's merry, and I can't imagine a better way to accomplish their goal."

"Oh, that is so wonderful! It is music to my ears," Willie said. He began to sob in gratitude, which made me want to do all I could to assist him in helping his orphans.

"I would like the furby back, since he is a non-functioning toy now anyway. I'm a little embarrassed to admit it, but I've grown emotionally attached to that ugly damn thing," I said, with a shy smile. "But I want to invite you and all the orphans to the Alexandria Inn, a bed and breakfast my husband and I own, for a holiday celebration on Christmas day. We will even have Santa Claus on hand passing out gifts to the children. As I've said before, 'the more the merrier!'"

"Oh my gosh! That would make their day, and mine too! That is so generous of you to offer. My wife passed away several years ago, and that's when I decided to dedicate my life to helping orphaned children. She and I were both orphaned at young ages. She was immediately adopted by her aunt and uncle, but I was passed from one foster home to the next, never having a family to call my own. I wanted to help prevent other children from having to suffer that same fate. My goal is to find a permanent home for every child in my care. So far I've helped get seventeen children adopted and into happy, loving families. That makes it all worthwhile to me."

"You are a remarkable individual, Mr. Cooper," I said. "Excuse my nosiness, but why is your home for sale?"

"I need the money to support the orphanage, and then I wouldn't have to hire help to run the home for me. It is a large, older estate I bought and renovated to house the children and an overseer. I will be happier living there anyway. I can be more involved with the kids there, so it would be a win-win situation all the way around. I hope I can afford to give up my security guard position, if at all possible, because they need a caregiver there at all times. The overseer has too many other responsibilities to kiss skinned elbows, and comfort children after they've experienced a nightmare or been the target of a bully at school."

"Well, I am going to set up a charity fund to help support the orphanage. With a little more promotion of the cause, I think we can get donations rolling in again," I vowed. "In the meantime, at least until your home sells and the donations begin coming in, we will help out with the bills as much as we can afford to."

"I'll pitch in what I can too," Wyatt said.

"I can afford to donate a portion of my income too," Detective Russell offered. "I'm not married yet, and have no family to support."

"Wow," Willie Cooper said. "This has become the worst and best day of my life. Who would have ever thought I would go from being arrested and looking at prison time, to seeing my dream come true, all in the matter of a few minutes? I can't thank you all enough. I will never be able to repay you all for your kindness."

"You can repay us by continuing your good work in helping those orphans find homes," I said. "And also by bringing your kids and their precious smiles to the inn on Christmas Day, to help make our holidays just that much brighter."

We dropped Willie off at his home. I collected Frank Furby and sat in the back seat holding him like a mother who'd just gotten her kidnapped child back safe and sound. I'm sure I was wearing my most self-satisfying facial expression. Had anyone else witnessed it, my smugness would have probably made them puke. But I could not be any happier with my idea to adopt the Allen family, Coral's family, and now the orphans, and to share our Christmas spirit with people who could not provide their own this holiday season.

CHAPTER 8

When Santa told me to sit on his lap and tell him what I wanted for Christmas, I didn't hesitate. I sat down, pulled his fake white beard down to kiss him, and said, "I want for all the children in the world to be as happy as these eleven kids here today are at this very moment."

We both sat silently for a few minutes watching the three Allen kids, Coral's son and daughter, and Willie's six orphans, as they laughed and played with all their new toys. They had been so wound up throughout our Christmas supper, that none of them ate enough to keep boll weevils alive. They were surely already operating on stored fat to have the energy they were all expending.

When Santa had asked them each what they wanted for Christmas, Seth and Hailey told him they wanted their father to come home for Christmas. It broke all of our hearts to have to deny them their one wish. Dax's wishes were easier to grant. He had squealed in delight when Stone handed him the motorized tank and collection of G.I. Joe action figures he'd requested. At four, he was too young to truly understand the situation, and what was happening around him. He just knew he was enjoying it tremendously.

As Dax began to play with his new toys, I wondered if he'd grow up and join the military as his father had. I could see the young boy one day serving to protect our freedom, as Blake Allen was doing on this very Christmas Day.

As expected, each and every one of the orphans wished for a family to call their own. Santa told them he would do his best to fulfill their requests before the next Christmas rolled around. Stone winked at Willie Cooper who was nodding in agreement. I knew this man would do all he could do to see that Santa's promise was kept. Watching Wendy and Andy's reactions to the children, I wondered if they'd someday marry, and maybe even adopt a child or two of their own.

Even I was taken by surprise when Santa stood up and announced he had one more surprise. He led the Allen children over to the couch and had them sit down. "It's not exactly what you asked for, kids, but it's the best we could do under the circumstances."

He introduced Andy as one of his elves when Stone's nephew walked into the room with a laptop computer. Andy sat the laptop down on the table facing the children and suddenly Blake Allen's face emerged on the monitor screen. The room erupted into cheers. A lone tear ran down my cheek as I watched the entire family's faces light up in pure joy.

It seems Andy had contacted Abbie's husband earlier in the week, and together they'd arranged for Blake to *skype* with his family over Andy's laptop. After the Allen family conversed for about ten minutes, sharing their love and Christmas wishes with each other, Blake had to end the skype session to report back to duty. I then reached under the tree to gather up the gifts our family had personally selected for all of our guests.

Both Abbie and Coral began to cry when they opened up their Kindles and Amazon gift cards, and the children opened up their new Xbox 360 gaming devices. I had returned to Best Buy to purchase one for the orphans, as well. Wrapping paper was flying everywhere, the children were laughing and shouting in glee, and we all were warmed by the glow on the faces of our large "adopted" family. I also handed Mr. Cooper a gift card worth a thousand dollars at Sam's Club to help stock up on food supplies to feed the six kids. He began to smile and weep at the same time. I had decided if I could waste that much money trying to track Willie Cooper down to have him arrested, I could afford the same amount to support his worthwhile endeavors, now that my investigative efforts had been successful. It was the best thousand bucks I'd spent in a long, long time.

It was at that very moment, I vowed to myself to volunteer to help collect toys for the Toys for Tots program every year. I could think of no better way to pay homage to our Lord on his birthday. And I'd make sure the orphanage received all the toys they needed, as well.

When, in the midst of total chaos, Seth Allen exclaimed, "This is the best Christmas ever," I could not have agreed more.

A few minutes later, it was clear that Andy, Wendy, Wyatt, and Veronica were as delighted as Stone and I were when each child in turn stepped up and gave each one of us a heart-felt hug and a handmade Christmas card they had created themselves.

I immediately put our cards up on the fireplace mantle, on either side of Frank Furby, who would be placed there every holiday season in the future to remind us of this most wonderful Christmas Day. Frank could no longer talk, sing, or dance, but I could swear he had a smile on his face, as he looked out over the room that was chock-full of holiday cheer, while we celebrated the spirit of the season at the Alexandria Inn.

Turn the page for an

excerpt from

JUST DUCKY

A Lexie Starr Mystery
Book Five

Jeanne Glidewell

"Name's Reliford," he answered, although it came out sounding more like "really bored" because of his current condition.

"Hmm, I knew a lady whose last name was Reliford before she got married a few years ago. Her name was Bertha. Poor lady was found dead in the library a couple days ago. Was she any relation to you?" I asked, innocently.

"Yeah, she was my old lady for a long, long time. Went by Bert, and now I hear she goes by Ducky. Always hated the name her mama give her. Too bad about the dying thing; heard she hung herself."

"Yeah, that's what the investigators said. She didn't seem like the suicide type to me, though. Did she to you?" I asked.

"Dunno. Never could figure that broad out, myself."

"Were you two still on good terms? When was the last time you saw her?"

"Ain't talked to Bert since the divorce was final," Bo said. He had drained his last beer in two or three gulps and opened up another bottle. He seemed in somewhat of a stupor, as he continued, "But I think I might have seen her in (hiccup) town a couple weeks ago. I pulled up behind a (loud juicy belch) VW bug at a light, and the driver looked like that old (very graphic adjective) bitch, so then I (incoherent muttering) so I could teach her a lesson."

"You must be very angry about the divorce. I'm sure you didn't deserve to be dumped that way," I said, hoping to get him stirred up and elaborating, no matter how crudely, on how he, in a drunken rage entered the library after I left, got involved in a heated argument with Ducky, or Bert, as he called her, and decided to drag her up the ladder and hang her from one of the log beams. Afterward, to save his own hide, he typed up a suicide note on one of the computers designated for library patrons to use, printed it out, and left it on the chair at her desk. That's what I hoped to hear and be able to decipher, amid all the hiccupping, belching, cursing, and even, occasionally, noxious farting. With all the sounds emitting from him, this old fellow was a one-man band.

If I could get him started confessing his sins, I would activate the voice recorder app on my smart phone, and then drive his recorded confession straight to the police station. I was very proud of the plan I'd developed, and was mentally patting myself on the back for a job well done. So naturally, I was then terribly disappointed when instead of reciting a detailed description of how he'd murdered his ex-wife, he merely passed out cold on the couch, dropping his nearly full beer on the linoleum floor.

Watching the beer flow out of the bottle onto the dark, grimy floor, creating a large puddle, the urge to urinate became more than I could control. As much as the thought disturbed me, using this man's *new-fangled crapper* had become a necessity. I'd used enough gas station restrooms in the past to perfect the art of peeing without one inch of my flesh ever touching the toilet seat, and I would have to utilize that talent again now.

When I was done relieving myself, I'd head home and leave Bo to sleep it off in his chair. There'd be no more conversing with him until he sobered up, and I needed to get home shortly anyway, to avoid worrying Stone.

I found the bathroom behind the second door down the hallway. The restroom was every bit as nasty as I'd imagined, but I'd have to risk untold germ and bacteria exposure, and use it. I locked the door behind me in case Bo woke up and came looking for me. Evaluating the toilet in front of me, I tried to imagine what bell or whistle it had that the old one might not have, and came up with nothing. Unless, I thought, it was the black mold under the lid, or the ring around the bowl a jackhammer couldn't chip off.

After peeing while performing a world-class balancing act, I realized there was no toilet paper on the holder. There was not even an old Sears catalog in the john. Thank God I carried a small pack of Kleenex in my fanny pack just for emergencies such as this one.

After completing the task at hand, I grasped the doorknob only to find it wouldn't unlock. I shook the rusty knob as violently as I could, jammed my fingernail file in the key opening, and wiggled it frantically. I then hollered out as loudly as I could, hoping to raise Bo. When those attempts failed, I looked for door hinges to remove the bolts from, but for some odd reason the door opened outward instead of inward, putting the hinges on the other side of the door.

My next thought was to crawl out the window, but was forced to accept the fact that, although I might be able to squeeze my arms and head out the tiny window, the extra junk in my trunk was going nowhere. Even if I busted out the window, and greased the window frame with oily residue off the floor, there was no hope of squeezing my rump and thighs through the opening.

Damn that Wyatt Johnston! If I didn't always have to keep so many fattening treats on hand to satisfy his sweet tooth, and then feel obligated to taste-test them before serving them to him, there might have been a prayer of escaping Bo's utterly disgusting privy.

I tried messing with the doorknob again, while intermittently calling out Bo's name, to no avail. Glancing at my watch, I knew it was Stone calling as soon as my phone rang. I could be evasive, or even downright lie about my situation, but what good would that do me at this point? It wouldn't get me out of the slimy, stinking bathroom anytime soon. I decided to bite the bullet and explain to him what had happened. I knew it would result in a lecture about my appalling disregard for my personal safety, and my lacking the sense God gave a lemming, on Stone's part, and a lot of shameless crying and pleading on mine, but it had to be done.

Apparently, Stone was getting accustomed to my impulsive nature, and the unfortunate and sometimes dangerous, predicaments this bad trait sometimes landed me in. He was angry, disgusted, and bitterly disappointed with me, but he didn't sound at all surprised. He sighed and asked for directions to Bo's place. Before he hung up, he asked, "This dude actually bought your story of being interested in buying his harrow?"

"Well, sure, I was very convincing. He even believed I might want to purchase his old toilet, since he done went and bought himself one of those new fangled crappers."

Stone didn't laugh, comment, or even sigh again. He just rudely hung the phone up in my ear. I could tell it was going to be a long, long night.

JUST DUCKY
available in
print and ebook

Jeanne Glidewell and her husband, Robert, live in Bonner Springs, Kansas. When not traveling or fishing in south Texas, Jeanne enjoys reading, writing, and wildlife photography. She's the author of *Soul Survivor,* and five Lexie Starr mysteries. A member of Sisters-in-Crime, she's working on more Lexie Starr mysteries. You may contact her through her website, www.jeanneglidewell.com.

Jeanne is a pancreas and kidney transplant recipient and volunteers as a mentor for the Gift of Life program in Kansas City. The promotion of organ donation is an important endeavor of hers. Please be an organ donor, because you can't take your organs to heaven, and heaven knows we need them here.

www.ingramcontent.com/pod-product-compliance
Lightning Source LLC
Chambersburg PA
CBHW022042170626
46808CB00003B/1326